WITHHOLD

WITHHOLD

MOSAIC CHRONICLES BOOK NINE

ANDREA PEARSON

This is a work of fiction, and the views expressed herein are the sole responsibility of the author. Likewise, characters, places, and incidents are the product of author's imagination, and any resemblance to actual persons, living or dead, or actual events or locales, is entirely coincidental.

Withhold, Mosaic Chronicles Book Nine

Copyright © 2016 Andrea Pearson

Book design and layout copyright © 2016 by Andrea Pearson
Cover copyright © 2016 Andrea Pearson, Shutterstock

All rights reserved. No part of this book may be reproduced or transmitted in any form or by any means whatsoever without written permission from the author, except in the case of brief quoatations embodied in critical articles and reviews.

Printed in the United States of America

ISBN-13: 978-1979337496
ISBN-10: 1979337497

SERIES BY ANDREA PEARSON

Kilenya Chronicles
Kilenya Romances
Kilenya Adventures
Mosaic Chronicles
Koven Chronicles
Ranch City Academy

DEDICATION

Helen Allred
For having an amazing eye—you always manage to find typos in books I think I've perfected. Thanks for beta reading and being a wonderful friend through the past many years.

Barb Hackel
For being warm, caring, and concerned over several years of trials for me and my family. I'll love you forever for your prayers and words of comfort!

CHAPTER ONE

Nicole sensed the Fire Pulser draw power toward herself, and she knew the creature was about to pulse flames again. She leaned against the rough bark of a nearby tree, taking mental stock of herself, and winced as injuries of varying degrees manifested themselves. There was no way she'd survive two or three more bouts of flames at this point.

She had to get to that glowing orb Lasia was guarding and find the fourth and final talisman before Keitus did. It was the only way to stop him from gaining enough power to control everyone. But how? She and Lasia had been grappling for at least thirty minutes now, and she was no closer to reaching her goal than when she'd first entered the forest. She couldn't bear to return to her friends empty-handed. Even now, two of them waited

WITHHOLD

just inside the library, probably restlessly, holding on to the hope that had motivated them all through the past several months of failures.

Keitus had constantly been a step ahead of them. He'd managed to secure the first three talismans through thievery and deception. Nicole would never forget the intense disappointment she'd felt when she and her friends had learned that the talismans they'd fought so hard to get had been *fakes*.

And now, here she was, facing an enemy who had nearly killed her only a couple of months earlier, and who would most likely kill her now. Nicole wasn't going down without giving her all to this task that had been appointed to her.

A sudden idea struck her, and she dashed through the forest to where she'd hidden the lantern. She wasn't exactly sure how it worked, but holding that lantern somehow caused the door to Shonlin to open, granting her access to this forest, and in turn, every magical item ever created.

After picking it up, Nicole ran back toward the Fire Pulser. Lasia hadn't moved an inch. She watched Nicole with confusion and suspicion from where she stood by the chest-high orb.

Not waiting to see what the Fire Pulser would do, Nicole tossed the lantern at the creature. Lasia caught it and stared at it, shocked just long enough for Nicole to tackle her into the glowing orb.

Visions sprang into Nicole's mind. She could no longer feel her pain or sense the Fire Pulser. Numbness blossomed over her, and her sight blackened for a moment. Then she saw a white glass box.

And Keitus.

The elderly man was surrounded by falling snow and pristine fields of white. Nicole could almost feel the crisp air as it puffed out of the old man's mouth. It wasn't her imagination when Keitus turned and looked at her, making eye contact. He laughed, obviously knowing where she was and what she was doing.

"You're too late," he said.

Keitus picked up the glass box, opened it, and pulled out the final talisman, tucking it into his pocket.

Nicole felt Lasia struggling against her grasp. The numbness in her body dissolved, and the vision ended. Her sight returned to the forest surrounding her and the Fire Pulser. Her heart sank—Keitus had what he needed. She was too late.

Lasia finally got a hand free. She punched Nicole in the jaw, nearly causing her to release her grasp, but Nicole didn't let go. The cord tying Lasia to the orb was magical. The Fire Pulser knew that without the cord keeping her in place, the forest wouldn't allow her to remain. Nicole was a guardian of Shonlin. A guardian over every magical item ever created, including Lasia's bindings. As such, she had access to the magic that would allow her to seal that cord in place.

Nicole closed her eyes and mentally pulled the necessary power to herself until it enveloped her, granting her permission to perform the act. She spoke the required words, and just like that, the cord was sealed, its magic rendered useless.

Lasia was free.

WITHHOLD

She screamed, and Nicole held on tightly as the magic of Shonlin realized a traitor was there. It dragged a shrieking Fire Pulser through the forest, banging the two women into underbrush, logs, and branches. The ferns pulled away from them. Lasia scrambled, struggled, and yelled.

Nicole had to put all of her energy into her grip. The beast pulsed multiple times, but each episode was weaker than the last. Still, Nicole felt her protection stop working and the burning start. She gritted her teeth against the pain.

Lasia was thrust back into the library, and Nicole was sucked through after her. She pinned the Fire Pulser to the stone floor, not sure what to do now that they'd left the forest.

The Fire Pulser froze and began glowing brightly, so bright that Nicole couldn't look directly at her. She scrambled to get away just before Lasia exploded into a million particles of light.

She shielded her eyes as bits of dust and glitter settled everywhere.

A wave of gratitude from hundreds of guardians who had been watching, waiting for Lasia to be removed from the forest, rushed over her.

Nicole glanced at the current guardian and asked, "Is that it? Has she been destroyed?"

He shook his head. "No, a council still must take place."

"What sort of council?" Nicole asked.

"You'll see."

The guardian didn't say anything more.

Waves of excruciating pain began rolling over Nicole. Pushing it all aside, she rushed through the door and out to where Akeno and Jacob waited in the next room near the balcony, overlooking the first floor.

"Nicole!" Akeno said. "Are you done?"

"Yes. We don't have much time. Can't stand around talking."

Jacob jumped to his feet. "But you're injured."

Nicole shrugged. It made her shoulders hurt, but she refused to let that distract her. "Doesn't matter. Keitus has all of the talismans. We're too late to stop him. We have to let everyone know."

"What do you mean, we're too late?" Akeno asked.

"He's got what he needs," Nicole said. "The talismans, the amulet—" She paused, glancing at Jacob.

"But not Helen's body," Jacob said.

Nicole smiled. "You're right."

The talismans could be joined with the amulet, but without a magical person's body, voluntarily given, it wouldn't do Keitus any good. "Now that we know he plans to destroy her, we might be able to convince her to tell him no."

CHAPTER TWO

ත ✦ ଓ

Nicole didn't wait to see if the others would follow. She rushed down the stairs of the library, trailing her hand on the railing as she went. The sound of footsteps behind her on the marble steps let her know they were coming.

Right before she reached the front of the library, the massive door swung inward, and Austin and Lizzie entered. Austin threw his arms around Nicole, burying his face in her neck. She cringed against the pain, not wanting to hurt his feelings by rebuking him.

"I'm so glad to see you," he said. "I was very worried."

Nicole kissed him on the cheek. "I know. We don't have much time."

"What's the hurry?" Lizzie asked.

"Keitus got to the fourth talisman before I could

defeat Lasia and find it myself. He has everything he needs, except Helen's body." She beckoned them to follow, then ran down the outer steps of the library and rushed to the street.

"Hold on!" Austin called. "We need to think this through."

"I have," Nicole said, pausing on the cobblestoned road. "And it's a race to see who can reach Helen first."

"How do we know he hasn't already talked to her?" Jacob asked, joining them.

"We don't," Nicole said, hopping from foot to foot, willing the conversation to end. "We need to assume he has. But if we don't do anything, if we don't try to stop him, we've already failed."

"Well, we have to figure out how to approach her," Austin said. "I mean, we can't just go running off to . . . to wherever she is." He folded his arms, staring at Nicole with his eyebrows raised. "Where were you going, anyway?"

"I . . ." Nicole hesitated. "Um . . . I'm not sure."

Austin half smiled. "Okay, so let's figure out where she was buried. That's the first step."

"And that would be in Washington somewhere," Lizzie said. "At least, that's where she tortured me the most."

Nicole tried to ignore the disappointment that cascaded over her. They were right—she hadn't even figured out where she'd go once she got out of Edana. And now that Keitus had the talismans, whatever advantage they may have had just slipped away. Would they ever catch up with him now? He had to know where Helen's

WITHHOLD

body was. And if he didn't, could they hope to find her before he did, or had all of their efforts been for naught?

Jacob started down the path. He called over his shoulder, "Let's get back to the castle and discuss this with my parents and Mr. Coolidge."

Everyone followed him, and Nicole contented herself with their slower-than-she-would-have-chosen pace. She was grateful that the trek that usually took a couple of hours still only took one, though.

Once they got to the castle, the king and queen were ready. They were waiting patiently, eager to hear what happened in Shonlin. After Nicole reported, they agreed that the best course of action would be to approach Helen's spirit and try to stop her from giving her body to Keitus. That would need to happen in Nicole's dimension of earth and not Jacob's, as Helen had been an Arete.

King Dmitri sent a message to Professor Coolidge, asking if he would like to be involved in this trip. Of course Professor Coolidge's response was yes. Then he reminded them that Renforth, the Shiengol, had wanted to go as well. Those who would be going on the expedition included Coolidge, Azuriah, Renforth, Nicole, Austin, and Lizzie.

Before everyone could get together, however, they needed to figure out where Helen was buried. Nicole, Lizzie, and Austin volunteered to do the research while the others prepared for the trek.

Jacob keyed the three to Austin's apartment after picking up Nicole and Lizzie's laptops. He said goodbye, then left, shutting the door behind him.

Nicole and Austin met eyes, and for the first time in

a while, Nicole wished Lizzie wasn't around. She and Austin needed to figure out their relationship. The last thing Austin had said to Nicole before she'd gone to confront the Fire Pulser had been a panicked proposal. Did he still want to marry her? She assumed he did, but didn't want to bring it up in front of their friend. And what if he was rethinking the proposal? What if he wanted more time before they tied the knot?

She and the others sat on the couches with their laptops and began the tedious research. They started with notable deaths around Lake Crescent, where Lizzie had encountered Helen, poring over online periodicals and newspapers. After an hour, though, they still hadn't found anything. They didn't even know when Helen had died. She'd been well-enough known and spoken about that Nicole had expected to find information about her grave almost immediately.

After taking a quick snack break, they decided they needed Helen's exact death date before continuing. It was just too difficult to get what they needed without it, even when they knew it had happened roughly halfway through the nineteenth century.

This meant a trip to Lake Crescent and the nearby cities to ask the locals what they knew about the legends.

Lizzie sent a quick text to Nate, Austin's roommate and the guy whose family she'd stayed with when she first encountered Helen. He responded almost immediately, saying that she, Nicole, and Austin were welcome to head up there as soon as they wanted to, and that they could stay as long as necessary.

"Should we drive or have Jacob key us?" Lizzie

WITHHOLD

asked.

"Jacob, definitely," Austin said.

Lizzie bit her lip. "Don't you ever feel bad about needing to use him so much? It's not like he doesn't have anything else to do."

"No, I don't," Austin said.

Nicole and Lizzie looked at him in surprise.

"He's as involved in this as we are. If we don't stop Keitus, he'll be just as enslaved as we will be. That's worth a bit of inconvenience."

Good point.

They ended up having Jacob key them and Professor Coolidge to Port Angeles, where they rented a car to drive the hour and half to the cabin by Lake Crescent. That way, they could get around whenever they needed to and not have to wait for Jacob.

Nicole felt weird, knowing that none of them were old enough to rent a car—she felt like they'd experienced enough in the past few years to give them a lifetime of experiences. It was Professor Coolidge who rented the car and drove them to the cabin. Lizzie sat up front with him, and Austin and Nicole sat in the back.

Nicole scooted over and leaned her head against Austin's shoulder, staring down at their entwined hands, wishing they'd get a moment alone to talk about his proposal. Had it been on purpose, or had he only said it because he was stressed and anxious about her fighting the Fire Pulser? He hadn't acted awkwardly since she'd returned—in fact, it was as if nothing had happened at all between them.

Regardless, she knew they would eventually get

married. She just didn't know when.

Judging by Lizzie's body language, Nicole could tell when they were nearing the cabin. Lizzie fidgeted, her gaze frequently went out the window, and her seatbelt loosened and tightened as she obviously pulled on it. Nicole knew this was hard for her friend who'd had prior dealings with Helen—awful ones—but she hoped it would be cathartic too.

Their welcome to the cabin was warm and open. Steph, Nate's mother, took them inside and showed them to their rooms. Nicole and Lizzie shared a simple but elegant one at the back of the cabin on the second floor. The window overlooked the forest below and gave them a breathtaking view of snow-capped mountains and in the distance and the nearby dark-green trees.

After dumping their things on the beds, the girls joined Austin and Coolidge in the small family dining room to eat a quick meal before heading back to Port Angeles. They wanted to get started as soon as they could. The food was delicious and the chatter friendly and light. Nicole was almost able to forget the tiredness she'd been experiencing since Akeno applied healing sap to her burns. She would have time to sleep later—finding Helen was more important.

Once they'd finished eating, the four of them hopped into the rental car and headed to Port Angeles, where they split up, dividing the city between Austin and Coolidge and Nicole and Lizzie. Nicole wished she could be with Austin, but knew that Lizzie would not be comfortable alone with their professor.

"I mean, he's kind of freaky," Lizzie said.

WITHHOLD

"Still?" Nicole asked. "We've been taking classes from and working with him for a while."

"I know, I know. It's just . . . Oh, never mind. I'm just being weird is all."

"No, you're not. I forget that you haven't spent as much time with him as I have."

The girls dropped the conversation to concentrate on their task. Nicole knew there used to be a cemetery in the middle of Port Angeles. She remembered reading that it was on Fifth Avenue and Oak Street, so they started knocking on doors there.

Most of the people who were home didn't know anything about anyone who had lived in Port Angeles over a hundred years earlier, but eventually they reached someone their age named Jill who was obsessed with family history. She invited them in and had them sit in a small sunroom off the main entrance before leaving to get something.

While waiting for Jill to return, Nicole inspected the sunroom. The windows were open, allowing in a fresh breeze. Flowerpots lined those windows, their colorful blossoms releasing pungent aromas that tickled Nicole's nose. The sunshine and warmth tried to envelop her in slumber, but she fought it off, fidgeting with her phone in her lap instead. The room reminded her of her mother's sunroom.

Jill returned, holding a box of old leather journals. "These were my great-great-grandmother's. She was Helen's neighbor."

She scanned through the journals, looking for mention of Helen. "I know I've seen it in here somewhere. If I can't find it, though, I know just the person to send you to." She glanced up at her visitors. "I'd send you now, but I'd like to help you as much as I can first."

After a moment, she finally found what she was looking for. It was an entry that talked about Helen and how she'd gone crazy. The girl read it, paraphrasing as she went.

"Okay, so apparently, Helen overdid her powers. It sounds like Sutherland, the man she was in love with, was trapping animals up in the mountains above Lake Crescent when he got attacked by a grizzly. Helen wasn't far away—it seems she was worried about him and stayed within easy walking distance of him whenever he was in town. Kinda stalkerish. Anyway, she heard his cries for help and dashed through the trees to stop the grizzly. Not having a weapon, she had to use her powers to get the bear to leave. It took a lot more magic than she'd ever used before, and it knocked her out. The grizzly was demolished completely."

"What happened after that?" Lizzie asked, totally involved in the story.

"Sutherland carried Helen off the mountain and into the town, where she remained unconscious for many weeks." Jill scanned several more entries. "Okay, so when she came to, she asked him if he would stay with her. He had to say no because he'd proposed to his beloved shortly before that trip, and his heart belonged to her."

Jill pulled out a picture of Sutherland and handed it to Lizzie, who glanced at it before passing it to Nicole.

Nicole studied it. He had long hair, a salt-and-pepper

WITHHOLD

beard, and totally looked like a fur trapper. Smile and worry lines creased his face. She couldn't stop staring at his eyes. They were kind, friendly, and approachable, but also sad. She was touched at how much emotion was visible in one picture.

Had this been taken before or after Helen went crazy? How did he *really* feel about her? He'd been engaged, but that didn't mean he hadn't ever returned her feelings.

Nicole handed the picture back. "Does it say whether he ever felt anything for her?"

"No, it doesn't." Jill read ahead. "When Helen woke up, she told him she would be there for him forever. She promised she'd return for him. And then she faded away—her personality, her sanity, everything. She began wandering the forest, searching for him.

"Unfortunately, she fell to her death from rocks on her family property. The rocks overlooked the strait where she'd watch for him to return. Her family buried her there."

Nicole didn't say anything for a moment. She sensed Lizzie's hesitancy to break the silence as well. "Does it say exactly where her grave is?" she asked finally.

Jill nodded. "The property belongs to the great-grandson of Helen's sister. He's a cranky old man and definitely not friendly."

"Do you think he'd let us see her grave?"

Jill hesitated. "Probably. But take care when you approach him—I'm not kidding when I say he's cranky."

She gave Nicole the address, and Nicole and Lizzie thanked her for her time, promising to return if they found any information she could add to her family history.

As soon as the girls were outside, Nicole pulled out her phone to call Austin.

"We've got it," she said. "Come get us and we'll head out there right now."

CHAPTER THREE

∽ ♦ ଔ

Everyone piled out of the car when they arrived at the man's house. The house was old, windblown, and had been painted white at one point. Most of that paint had peeled off. Shutters hung at the windows, a couple of them waving in the wind, creaking, not fully fixed to the house anymore. Dead vines clung to one half of the small, one-story place, and dead rosebushes lined the walk.

The gate was wide open, and they approached the house cautiously. Something was off. It felt vacant. Nicole gathered her powers, sensing as the others did the same.

The front door was open a crack. A chair lay on its side, the back of it broken, and pieces of it strewn on the old carpet where it had fallen. It looked like someone or something had been in a fight.

They didn't even bother knocking before entering—it was obvious the place was empty. Their quick search of the house was over in seconds.

Nicole glanced at the others. "What should we do?"

Coolidge returned her gaze, his expression troubled. "Maybe we should look out back, head toward the bluffs if we can't find anyone."

The others agreed. There wasn't a back door, so they went out front and headed around that way. Nicole gasped when she saw a crumpled body on the back porch. The rancid stench in the air suggested that whoever it was had been dead for some time. Flies buzzed, and the air in the semi-enclosed porch was heavy enough to make Nicole gag. She only got close enough to see a shriveled old man and to see that the skin on his face was bruised and his hair was falling out. His hands and feet were missing, and the jeans he wore had holes in them. Maggots were visible through those holes.

Nicole's stomach clenched, and she turned away, trying to minimize the air she breathed.

"Is that him?" Lizzie asked, her voice shaking.

The frown on Coolidge's face deepened. "I would assume so."

"Murder?" Austin asked.

"Given the circumstances, again, I would assume so." Coolidge didn't take a step closer to confirm, and no one else was willing to examine the body.

Austin ran his hand through his hair. "I'll call the cops," he said. "You guys go on ahead."

Nicole and Lizzie glanced at each other. Nicole didn't want to leave Austin alone to do the unpleasant

WITHHOLD

task, but she also didn't want to stick around the dead body. She'd seen enough of those to last her a couple hundred lifetimes.

Coolidge started down the tiny path, and the girls followed. It wound through the grass and weeds that consumed most of the backyard. A forest was up ahead, the trees short, brown, and scraggly—unusual for this location. Most of the other foliage they'd seen had been lush and green. These trees looked like they'd been starving for years. Maybe that was true—they *were* close to the salt water in the Strait of Juan de Fuca. But Nicole didn't know enough about gardening to figure out if being near the strait would make them shriveled.

The little path led them into the forest, where the air was cool, still, and calm. No animal noises reached Nicole, and the wind didn't brush the trees. The feeling there was one of reverence, almost sacredness. The juxtaposition of that with the health—or lack of it—of the trees bothered Nicole.

The forest ended right at the edge of the bluffs that overlooked the strait. Rather than admiring the beautiful view, Nicole and the others began searching for the grave. It wasn't difficult to find. A white cross with the word "Helen" etched into it was stuck in the ground, slanting to the right. Nicole's heart fell when she saw that the grave was open, the body gone, and no sign of the coffin. She shouldn't have been surprised—with the man dead, what else could she have expected?

Coolidge grumbled to himself. He knelt on the dirt next to the open grave, holding his hand over the hole, eyes closed. His magic snaked away from him, and

Nicole felt it question the surrounding elements, asking about Helen and her body. Coolidge held still for a long time, his brows furrowed.

After several moments, he got to his feet, wiping his hands on his pants. "She's not here. Her spirit is no longer connected to her body, and even if it were, we wouldn't find it here."

"What now?" Lizzie asked.

"We're going to have to go to the dimension of bones to find Helen. That's most likely where she resides now."

Nicole and Lizzie nodded. Nicole couldn't help but wonder why most Aretes went there after death. It wasn't exactly a "rest in eternal bliss" place. She found herself relieved to know that when she died, she would be in Shonlin for a while. There was some comfort in that.

"I wish we had Anna Morse to help us," she said. The old woman had been destroyed when the Great Ones had come to earth a year earlier.

"We'll use Robert instead," Coolidge said.

Nicole had almost forgotten about her professor's friend who had passed away the same time Anna Morse had. He'd helped them before, when they'd been searching for Keitus's place.

The three of them walked back to the deserted house. Austin was still on his phone, maintaining a healthy distance from the body, a serious expression on his face.

Realizing they would have to wait until the cops arrived, Nicole and Lizzie headed around front to the porch swing. They hopped onto it, kicking against the sagging wood on the porch to get moving.

"Awful luck," Lizzie said.

WITHHOLD

"Seriously." Nicole sighed. "Nothing is ever simple."

They waited in silence until the police arrived, then they escorted the officers around back.

After answering questions, Nicole and her friends were finally able to leave. She wished she knew more about the man who had died. It was obvious that he'd been killed by Keitus's men. What was his name? What was his story? Her heart ached, thinking about his situation. How long had he been dead? And how had no one else found him? He must have been alone. She hoped he would find peace in the next world. Regardless of how cranky he was, he didn't deserve to die at the hands of an evil man and his minions.

They dropped the car off at the rental place, and Jacob picked them up and keyed them back to Seattle.

Austin followed the girls home so they could gather their stuff. Lizzie needed help studying for a Fire test, and Austin had volunteered. It was a great opportunity for Nicole to practice as well, since she still hadn't mastered all of Water or any of Fire.

They headed to Austin's apartment. Nate wasn't there yet, but he promised he would come as soon as he dropped his girlfriend off at her place. He was a Fire Arete and had progressed a lot recently, and Nicole looked forward to seeing what she could learn from him. The girls and Austin got comfortable on the couch while waiting, discussing what Nicole and Lizzie needed to work on.

"My biggest goal this semester...and possibly next," Lizzie started, "is to learn how to stop Fire completely."

"That's going to be fairly difficult," Austin said.

"Especially since your native ability is to start it."

Lizzie nodded. "I know. Nicole told me. But I'm determined, and who's to say I can't figure it out?"

"Don't worry," Austin said. "I have no doubt you'll master it."

Lizzie grinned. "Maybe not easily," she said. "But hopefully easier with you and Nicole helping me."

Once they'd discussed everything, they waited for a few moments more, each content in his or her own thoughts, and Nicole found herself glancing at her phone several times. Where was Nate? Should she ask Lizzie to leave so she and Austin could talk in private?

Would it bother or relieve him if she brought up the proposal topic? Regardless, the conversation would be better if it happened in private, so Nicole put the topic from her mind and relaxed against the back of the couch, staring at the ceiling.

Nate finally got home, and the four of them gathered around the counter in the kitchen to start working on their abilities. Nate's was to grow fire, not to start it or stop it. So Lizzie created the fires, Nate made them grow, and then Lizzie worked on stopping them.

Nicole could tell how frustrated her best friend was at this exercise. She was only able to stop a fire that was the size of a small candle. Nicole could barely sense Fire at the very edge of her conscience. Instead of pushing herself too much, she started working on Water instead, gathering the molecules of moisture from the air. She concentrated on making that water expand.

After half an hour, she held enough water with her powers that it coated the upper half of the room. With a grin of triumph, she let it fall into the sink—being careful not to get anyone wet—and smiled at the expression of pride on Austin's face.

Lizzie slumped in her chair, staring at the now-wet sink. "It's not fair."

"You'll get it," Nicole said. "Besides, I still can't do *anything* with Fire. You're way ahead of me where that's concerned."

Lizzie nodded. Then, with a sigh, she delved into practice again. Nicole decided to see if she could learn from her best friend—sense how Lizzie was creating Fire. She commanded her magic to follow Lizzie's, hoping to glean some information. She felt as Lizzie reached out with her powers, but could only follow along for a short while. Fire was simply outside of her grasp.

Nicole was frustrated with her lack of progress in that area, but she was being unfair to herself, especially since she hadn't fully mastered Water yet. She couldn't master Fire until she understood Water. Instead of forcing herself to practice with Water again, though, she relaxed and enjoyed her time with two of her most favorite people.

After two hours, everyone decided they were ready for a break. Nate headed for dinner at his girlfriend's apartment while the others chose to go explore Seattle. Nicole couldn't believe she'd lived there for over two years and hadn't really gotten to know the city itself.

"Where should we go?" Nicole asked.

"I know just the place!" Lizzie said, practically bouncing. "It's called Ye Olde Curiosity Shop. It's a little store down by Elliot Bay that I discovered while you guys were off on one of your adventures. It's got all sorts of cool things in it, including mummies, shrunken heads, petroglyphs, totally real totem poles, and all sorts of other awesome stuff."

Nicole raised an eyebrow. "Shrunken heads? Yeah, I'm not sure how I feel about that."

Lizzie giggled. "You can ignore that part. But just wait and see. The place is freaking awesome."

After everyone agreed to give the store a try, they piled into Austin's car and drove to Alaskan Way, where it was located. Stepping inside the shop, Nicole knew right away that Lizzie was right. This was a place they *had* to explore. It was cramped and crowded and smelled a bit musty, but she fell in love immediately. The shop was full of some seriously crazy stuff. A four-legged chicken, shrunken heads, the Lord's Prayer on a penny, and many other things that totally caught her off guard. Her favorite, of course, were the mummies—Sylvester and Sylvia.

Realizing they wouldn't have nearly enough time to explore everything in the store, Nicole bought a book called *A Curious Alphabet* that listed twenty-six fascinating items that were housed there.

While they were browsing, Coolidge called Austin. The conversation was quick and Austin ended the call, then tucked his phone into his pocket, looking at the girls. "Robert is ready to talk to Helen, and Jacob is on his way."

CHAPTER FOUR

෨ ✦ ෬

"So, does Jacob know how to get here?" Nicole asked.

"Yes, I told Coolidge where we are. He told me to tell Sylvester hi for him."

Nicole and Lizzie laughed as they walked with Austin to the door, where Jacob was waiting. He explained that Renforth and Azuriah had decided not to come. Then he took them on a brief detour to Coolidge's house to get supplies, including food and water.

"We've got a long walk," Robert said once they'd met up with him. "It took me quite some time to figure out where this woman is, and it's not close."

"We're grateful you were able to find her," Nicole said. "We were worried that she wouldn't be here at all."

Robert glanced at Nicole. "She's here all right. I'm afraid she won't be very happy to see us, though."

He turned away, obviously not wanting to talk about

that anymore, so Nicole didn't chase the topic. She started to fret, though. What would make a *ghost* nervous?

They started out across the vast bleached-white hills and mountains of Anna Morse's dimension, the brittle bones crunching under their feet. Nicole couldn't wait until the day when she wouldn't ever have to return to this dimension again.

She hoped they would reach Helen in time to convince her to ignore Keitus and do what was right for everyone rather than what she felt was right for her situation.

Instead of taking them in the direction of Keitus's previous place, Robert led them to the left and through a narrow canyon. They passed through many small canyons after that. Nicole was glad they brought food, which she munched on as they walked.

The farther they went, the more she noticed an acrid smell in the air. It both tickled and burned her nose, making her sneeze several times.

Robert glanced back at her with a knowing expression. "That smell gets worse—much worse."

Nicole didn't need him to tell her that—she was already starting to notice it. "What is it?"

"You'll see soon enough. We should conserve energy just in case she attacks and not talk."

They traipsed through one more canyon, coming upon what looked to be a vast expanse of water. No mountains were in sight. A lone island, only a couple of feet above the water level, was visible in the distance.

As they continued toward the body of water, Nicole noticed that the bones underfoot began feeling softer. They started sticking to her shoes, making her calves

WITHHOLD

tire. Her feet were getting heavy.

"Be careful not to let the bones touch your skin," Robert said. "The stuff they're melted with is poisonous."

Nicole didn't need to be told twice. She wouldn't have touched them anyway, but it was good to have the warning regardless.

The closer they got to the water, the more Nicole realized it *wasn't* water. It was sludgy, thick, and grayish, like unset concrete. "What is it made of?" she asked when Robert stopped to survey it.

"Melted bones," he said. "And we have to cross it. She lives on the island."

"How do we get to her?" Coolidge asked. "We weren't prepared for this."

Robert jerked his thumb over his shoulder. Nicole and her friends glanced that way and saw several bones that had been tied together to form a raft.

Coolidge, Austin, and Robert grabbed the raft and dragged it toward the edge of the liquid ash. While the men were pulling the craft, Nicole and Lizzie gathered a bunch of very long bones that could work as poles to push with. Nicole hoped they'd be strong enough to get her and the others to the island and back safely.

Once everyone was on the small raft, Robert and Austin pushed off from the shore while Coolidge, Nicole, and Lizzie used their poles to guide the craft toward the island.

As Nicole expected, the raft moved slowly through the sludge. She glanced into it, unable to see anything inside whatsoever. "What's keeping this stuff from melting the boat?"

Robert looked at her, his expression serious. "Nothing."

Oh, great.

"But it should hold us until we talk to Helen and return."

Coolidge looked at his friend. "It *should* hold us?" he asked, an incredulous expression on his face.

"That's the plan," Robert said. "It's the best I could do—there isn't exactly an unlimited supply of wood or metal here."

"I suggest we go as fast as we can," Austin said.

If Nicole didn't feel so uneasy about their situation, she would've chuckled at the obviousness of Austin's statement. Instead of responding, though, she and Lizzie took on one side of the craft with Austin while Coolidge and Robert manned the other side. With long pushes, they slowly moved through the murky waters.

As they approached the island's shore, Nicole could see a lone figure standing straight and very still, facing away from them. She dropped her voice and whispered, "Is that her?"

Robert's yes barely reached her ears, and the already quiet group grew even quieter as they pushed toward the shore.

Helen was dressed in tattered, light-gray robes. A dark shawl covered her head. She appeared to be unmoving, her arms wrapped tightly around her waist, her head slightly bowed. What was she doing? Nicole's sense of unease increased as they approached. With a slight splatter of the liquid they floated on, they got the craft up onto the shore and laid their long poles on the bone-covered ground before huddling into a group to discuss who should approach Helen first.

"I vote I go," Robert said. "I'm the only one she can't really harm."

No one argued with him, and the others watched as he approached Helen cautiously. Before he'd even reached her, her shoulders began trembling slightly, and the sound of wailing drifted across the air. Was she crying? It seemed so. It wasn't surprising, given her history.

The cloud-covered sky seemed to darken, and Nicole found herself wishing for fire. She didn't dare ask Lizzie to light one, though. Not this close to a mentally unstable person who was so magically powerful. Especially not knowing Helen's current frame of mind.

Helen startled as Robert approached. She didn't turn around, but the wailing grew in volume, and Nicole met Lizzie's gaze. She prayed things would turn out okay for them. The woman's shoulders shook as she visibly sobbed, her back to the group.

The crying got even louder as Robert continued trying to converse with her. She didn't respond to him—didn't even acknowledge his presence, other than crying harder. Giving up, Robert joined the group, shrugging.

"Austin and I'll try now," Coolidge said.

The two men approached the woman, and with a sinking heart, Nicole realized something. The chances of any of them being able to convince Helen were slim. She wasn't normal—her mind wasn't in a place where she'd understand why they needed her help.

The moment Austin and Coolidge were close enough for Helen to sense them, her wailing increased in volume even more. Nicole felt a sudden pulse of magic growing, giving only a slight warning before it blasted them, knocking them all to the ground.

Helen finally turned, and Nicole gasped at the expression on her face, barely visible from where she'd fallen. It wasn't just anger and torment that caught Nicole off guard, but also the woman's eyes themselves. They were depthless—hollow.

Her soul was already gone.

CHAPTER FIVE

※ ♦ ※

The ground beneath them vibrated, and Nicole and the others jumped, glancing around. What was happening?

"Wave!" Robert shouted, pointing beyond Helen.

Nicole looked in that direction. A smudge on the horizon appeared near the opposite edge of the island. It grew larger and larger. Robert was correct—it was a massive wall of sludge heading straight toward them. Coolidge and Austin froze before managing to jump to their feet just in time. Combining their magic, not even needing to talk to each other to know what the other was doing, they pushed forward with their hands. The wave parted as it reached Helen and Nicole's group. The sludge raged overhead and on either side.

Coolidge and Austin called out to Helen, trying to reassure her that they were friends and not enemies, telling her they wanted to help with her situation with Keitus.

Nicole barely caught every other word.

The sound of the liquid became deafening as more and more of it waved over them, and Nicole could no longer hear anything the men were saying. From the looks of it, they weren't having any success. Helen was still shrieking, her mouth wide open in a continual scream and her eyes narrow with hatred.

Helen grew frustrated when she realized her efforts weren't stopping the people trying to talk to her. The woman increased the amount of magic she was flooding toward them, and Nicole realized with shock that she, being completely unhinged as an Arete, didn't have a limit on the amount of power she could expand. She'd already gone completely insane—expelling too much magic wouldn't cause any more damage than she'd already experienced.

Not only that, but she was dead, and Nicole and most of those accompanying her were alive. This woman had nothing to lose, but they did.

Nicole *had* to do something. The men were struggling, failing. Their magic was running out, bringing them to dangerous thresholds. She quickly sent her own magic, forcing the wave to continue flowing around them, using her ability to control air to envelop everyone and keep them in a pocket, safe from Helen's attacks. Then she jumped forward, passing the men. She stopped five feet away from Helen and tried to yell loud enough for the woman to hear her.

Helen was sobbing frantically, tears pouring down her face, her whole body shaking. Nicole raised her hands in a comforting "I bring peace" gesture. "Helen, please let us help you."

WITHHOLD

She wished she knew what to say—wished she knew what trigger words would get the woman to listen to her.

"You don't have to do this!"

Helen didn't respond. Her empty eyes stared somewhere beyond Nicole, her screams and sobs still undying.

After two more attempts, Nicole knew just how fruitless their efforts were—how doomed they'd been from the start. Helen was completely insane. She wasn't there anymore. She no longer had the ability to recognize friends or foes.

How had Keitus reached her when no one else could?

With a sick feeling, Nicole saw the answer. He'd promised Helen something she'd *never* get back again. And for a moment, Nicole actually understood the woman's motivations. Keitus promised to reunite her with her lover—he must have. All it would take was her body. And she would obviously be willing to give that up, since she'd lost it long ago when she'd fallen to her death.

Nicole sensed as her magic began to diminish. Grabbing Lizzie's arm—she hadn't even heard her friend screaming next to her—they ran back toward the men who were struggling to stay on their feet.

The massive wave gained power as they all ran away from Helen. Nicole pressed forward with her shield, commanding it to envelop the craft, forcing the gunk off the craft's surface and the poles. Only three of the poles remained. The men grabbed them, and everyone jumped onto the raft. Nicole felt helpless, watching as the men did all the heavy lifting, but she knew she wouldn't be able to use her magic *and* push them forward through the thick liquid.

Kneeling on the craft, lowering her head to her hands,

Nicole concentrated as hard as she could on her task of protecting them until they reached the other side. She sensed as Lizzie and Robert's magical pulses joined hers, strengthening her, giving her the ability to continue when she didn't have anything left to draw upon.

They finally reached the shore just as Nicole's powers gave out. Obviously sensing her struggle, Robert took up the bubble she had created and continued protecting them from the mountain of sludge that still crashed around them.

Knowing that Robert was a Fire Arete and wouldn't be able to control Air for very long, Nicole hoped her powers would recharge themselves quickly.

The five raced back through the canyons and around hills, still trying to outrun Helen's wave. That woman was *powerful*.

The wave finally began subsiding as they neared the door Jacob would Key them through. Whether Helen sensed they'd finally left her alone or because her power really did have limits, Nicole didn't know. She was simply grateful that the wave couldn't seem to reach the building itself.

Everyone dropped in exhaustion on the bones near the door. Jacob came through the link a split second later, a panicked expression on his face.

"That was really close," he said. "I was worried you wouldn't make it back."

"So were we . . . Jacob," Nicole gasped. "So were we."

CHAPTER SIX
☙ ✦ ❧

Right before everyone followed Jacob through the link back to earth, Austin grabbed Nicole's arm, holding her back. "Nicole, I've been patient, but I can't wait any longer. Before you left to fight the Fire Pulser, I asked an important question, and I've been—"

Nicole's heart had begun warming while Austin spoke, her toes and fingers tingling. He hadn't been regretting his proposal. But then the warmth in her heart grew more intense and she coughed, hitting her chest, realizing the heat wasn't entirely originating from her emotions.

A vision popped into her mind and she stumbled, knocking into Austin, feeling as his hand kept her steady. She saw the inside of the library, specifically the room tucked into the corner of the fifth floor. The current Shonlin guardian was there, his eyes open, watching her.

"Shonlin guardians," he said, "Onyev is calling. You

will have a brief moment to finish what you are doing before the magic of our realm pulls you away. Please emotionally prepare yourselves for a journey to the ancient Makalo city."

The vision ended, and Nicole's sight returned to the bone dimension and Austin. He was staring at her with concern. She coughed again, grateful that the heat was fading, and said, "I think the council for Lasia is about to take place. I just received a notice that Onyev is calling me and the other guardians back to the ancient Makalo city."

"How much time do you have?" Austin asked. If he was disappointed, he didn't show it.

"Not much. We'll talk when I get back, if that's okay."

She could already feel herself being pulled away. She panicked for a moment, trying to hold on to him harder. But with a deep breath, she forced herself to relax and let go.

Nicole appeared on the outskirts of a massive forest with trees that were similar to the ones in Gratitude City but bigger, broader, if that was even possible. They were dead and old. Most of them, even though huge, were withered and twisted. The landscape on the outskirts of the forest was desolate, the sky bleak.

Evidence that people once lived in this forest speckled the area—little wooden huts here and there, broken glass sparkled on the path near her feet, and some of the trees had cuts in them that obviously hadn't been made by nature. Above and beyond that, the feeling that permeated the air was one that she'd only ever sensed

WITHHOLD

from ghost towns and ancient ruins. Someone—probably many someones—had called this place home.

Jacob once told her that Makalos used to live separate from each other in a city made of trees—one Makalo per tree. They were unhappy that way, so they left. Was this that city? And if so, why had she been brought to it? Perhaps Shonlin brought her to the place where Onyev lived when he'd created it.

If this place had once been beautiful, it definitely wasn't now. It felt as if it had been frozen in time right after the mass exodus that had caused the trees to die. Nicole was alone. Where were the other guardians? And why had she been transported here and not to the meeting place?

Perhaps the city had a block on it that prevented magic from happening within it. If that was the case, she'd probably appeared as close to the meeting place as possible.

Nicole decided to enter the forest. She stepped forward cautiously, carefully, her feet falling on damp leaves that covered the path. The place was quiet—not even the sound of animals reached her ears. She had no desire to break the near reverence.

As she walked around the trees, following the narrow path, Nicole couldn't help but stare at their trunks. Right at the place where branches would normally begin, there were shallow holes about a foot wide, with several small tree branches webbing together to create the back and sides. What could those be for? From what she could see, all of the largest branches connected to that hole in some way. The farther she went, the larger the trees and their holes got.

She glanced into the next whole and shrieked. It had someone in it. She froze, her hand over her heart, and stared at the Makalo. He didn't move. His arms and legs were stretched out, his hands and feet disappearing into the branches. His hair was long, entwined in twigs. His eyes were open, staring ahead.

Nicole stepped to the side. The eyes didn't follow. They were glazed over, unseeing.

Nicole couldn't help it. She took a step closer. What happened to him? Did he die when the forest died, frozen in place, his body unable to rot away? Why didn't the other Makalos help him when they left? Or was he already dead by then?

An expression of sadness was on the creature's face, and she wondered if he'd chosen to stay behind, if he'd chosen not to follow Onyev's counsel.

One odd thing—there wasn't a stench accompanying him. Actually, nothing in the forest smelled. No rotted wood, no dirt, nothing. It was almost like the place was sterile.

Nicole rubbed the back of her neck, glancing one last time at the Makalo before continuing deeper into the forest. She saw a couple more bodies, but mostly the holes were empty. She was grateful for that.

Soft voices ahead finally reached her ears, filtering through the trees. For a time, the forest had been getting darker as the trees grew closer together. But now, a light gleamed through those trees, reaching her, warming her. Nicole increased her pace, eager to get out of the gloomy and creepy forest and to see someone alive.

WITHHOLD

She entered a large clearing and gasped. Onyev was stuck to a tree in the center, his hands, feet, hair, and beard entwining with the branches that surrounded the hole. Sadness was on his face. Why was he there? Was this where he created Shonlin?

The Makalo patriarch looked up and saw Nicole, sending her a tired smile before motioning to an empty spot on the ground.

Nicole was shocked that he could pull his hand away from the branches, but perhaps she shouldn't have been. She already knew the Makalos left of their own free will.

For the first time, she noticed that the clearing was full. She looked at the surrounding creatures as they looked at her. Even a Molg was there. Azuriah wasn't present—she guessed that was due to the fact that he was a future guardian, and only past or present ones were in attendance.

Nicole tried to calculate how many guardians there were, but gave up as she surveyed the variety of species present. How was it possible that all of these people had interacted with the Great Ones at some point during their lives? How many years had passed since Onyev had created Shonlin, anyway?

She didn't have much opportunity to think over her questions because moments after she sat down, Onyev called everyone to order, then asked for Lasia to be brought out.

CHAPTER SEVEN

A handful of humans brought a kicking and screaming Lasia into the clearing. Her arms were tied up with the same kind of cord that Keitus had used to attach her to the orb. How ironic. Why wasn't she pulsing flames? Nicole could sense the power coming from her, so why wasn't she using it? Did the magical block here allow Lasia to maintain her magic, but not use it?

The humans held Lasia a few paces away from Onyev. He flicked his hand, and roots shot from the ground, snaking up her legs before covering her almost entirely. Lasia shrieked, staring down, panicking. When the roots stopped moving, only her face was visible.

The clearing filled with murmuring and mumbling as the guardians watched Lasia with disappointment and anger. Nicole jumped when the current guardian appeared next to her, taking a seat.

WITHHOLD

He glanced at her, his eyes open. "The vines won't allow her to tell a lie while she's held by them. She'll be destroyed if she tries."

Onyev raised a hand, and silence fell across the group. "Lasia, you know the purpose of the roots that hold you in place. Do you understand what will happen if you try to lie?"

Lasia nodded. "Yes."

Onyev sighed, the lines of sadness on his face deepening. "Please tell us what you have done."

Lasia glared at him. "I agreed to grant Keitus access to Shonlin through me, thereby giving him the talismans."

"Why would you do this?"

Lasia flushed. "He made promises to me."

Onyev nodded, obviously expecting that. "What sort of promises?"

Lasia struggled to answer, and the vines tightened around her. She finally blurted out, "Family. He would grant me children of my own."

Murmurs filled the clearing as the guardians looked at each other in confusion.

Lasia turned her glare on the people around her. "You beasts," she spit out. "Able to breed so easily. Able to have children! My people are dying, and there's nothing I can do about it!" Her frown deepened, and the vines pressed against her as they sensed she had more to say. She blurted, "Keitus promised he'd mate with me."

Bile flowed up from Nicole's stomach, making her taste bitterness at the back of her mouth. Why would anyone *want* to mate with him?

Lasia continued. "Fire Pulsers live longer than

humans—our children would outlive him. *My* children would rule the worlds."

Onyev shook his head. "Lasia, you do realize that Keitus is already dead, do you not? If he isn't stopped, he will reign forever. *Nothing* will outlast him."

Lasia grounded her teeth. "He promised me Shonlin."

Onyev closed his eyes. He didn't respond for a moment. "You have placed countless people in jeopardy, and that is unpardonable. Keitus *never* would have granted those wishes. He doesn't share power, not even with his most loved and trusted associates."

The Makalo patriarch looked out at the guardians. "Even with Lasia's confession, our laws still demand testimony from any and all witnesses. We only have one. Nicole. Come, tell us what happened."

Nicole got to her feet and stepped forward to stand before Onyev. She quickly summed up her experiences with Lasia, how the Fire Pulser had attacked her every time she tried to find the final talisman.

"How did she handle being removed from the forest?" Onyev asked.

"She was definitely angry, and she didn't want me to stop her. She openly told me that Keitus had offered more than I or anyone else could give her. And she did everything in her power to destroy me. Once I'd gotten rid of the rope keeping her in place, she made sure I know she was irritated." Nicole lifted the back of her shirt, where the burns and scratches she'd received from being dragged across the forest were still healing. "I got these when I helped rid the forest of Lasia."

Onyev looked at the other guardians. "Does anyone

WITHHOLD

feel the need to defend Lasia?"

Those present fell completely silent. All eyes were on Onyev.

"Guardians," Onyev said, "converse amongst yourselves."

Nicole gasped as a sudden vision entered her mind. She and the other guardians were alone, standing in a tranquil meadow near a brook. No one said anything for several moments. Apparently, everyone was just as surprised, and no wonder—this had never happened before.

The current guardian stepped into the center, getting the others' attention. "It is my will that Nicole take charge of our debate. She is the current living guardian, and it is she who defeated Lasia."

Nicole flushed as the other guardians agreed and turned toward her. She wasn't sure what to do. This meeting within a meeting felt unnecessary. Perhaps it would be needed, in cases where there were witnesses voicing belief in the person accused.

"Well, we've all heard Lasia's account," Nicole said. "And Onyev obviously feels she's guilty." She took a breath, thinking. "Maybe I should ask if anyone thinks Lasia is innocent?"

No one raised a hand.

"Who believes that what she did was wrong?"

Every hand went up—there wasn't a doubt in the group about Lasia's guilt. As soon as that thought went through Nicole's mind, the vision ended, and they were back in the clearing with Onyev and the Fire Pulser.

Onyev looked across his guardians, and Nicole felt a

brief touch of his mind on hers.

"The verdict has been reached." He looked at Lasia, no emotion on his face. "Lasia, you are guilty. I strip you of your access to Shonlin. I strip your memory of everything you learned about the magical items protected there. I strip from your mind the knowledge of the locations of any magical item not contained within Shonlin. You are forthwith banned from interacting with guardians or anyone who owns or has the power to create a magical item."

Nicole sensed it when her bond with the Fire Pulser—a bond she didn't even know existed—was destroyed. Onyev reached outwardly and closed his eyes. The roots that held Lasia in place covered her completely, and with a swirling of wind and magic, Lasia disappeared. The vines that covered her fell to the ground, dead.

Onyev looked at his guardians again. "Lasia has been sent to another dimension—a prison dimension where she'll remain for the rest of eternity, or until her soul is destroyed." He took a breath. "I am grateful to say that no one else will betray Shonlin. It is incredibly heart-wrenching to know that even one of my beloved guardians turned against us."

Instead of excusing everyone as Nicole expected, Onyev turned to her. "As a thank you for what you've done for Shonlin, Nicole, I permanently seal to you the Kona Sphere."

Something burned lightly in Nicole's hand. She looked down, raising it. A little marble-shaped object was glowing bright gold in her palm.

"The Kona Sphere will never part from you, and it

will always appear when you need it."

The ball blinked brighter gold, then became translucent and started floating. Nicole watched in wonder as it hovered in front of her face.

"Dismiss the sphere," Onyev said. "You can do so in your thoughts—it hears you."

Nicole asked the little ball to go away, and it disappeared.

"It will always be with you—just call it when you need it."

Nicole wasn't sure what to say. She didn't even know what the sphere would do.

Onyev smiled, probably sensing her thoughts. It was the first happy look she'd seen on his face the entire time she'd been in that meadow. "The Kona Sphere is a replica of Shonlin. Among other things, it grants you access to information about magical items still there, without you having to travel to the library. It only works with items sealed there—to find objects not in the library, you will still need to visit the Shonlin forest."

He continued. "Even if you die, the Kona Sphere will stay with you. It will accompany you to the spirit world."

Nicole raised her eyebrows. That was pretty awesome. She suspected that she would probably end up in the bone dimension—no one had told her so, but it made sense, as other Aretes had gone there after death. Having the sphere with her would be pretty awesome.

"Thank you so much."

"You definitely deserve it," Onyev said. He glanced over everyone. "You're all excused."

Nicole turned to leave, but Onyev motioned for her to

wait. She joined him as the other guardians left the forest. Once they were alone, Onyev said, "I've never gifted this to anyone for a fairly large reason. I'm stronger than any who could guard it, but I sense that will be changing soon as you come to your powers. I'm no longer able to keep it safe—my magic wanes as I age. After everything you've done, I know you're trustworthy. The amount of power the Kona Sphere gives its owner is high—many would let it go to their heads.

"The sphere will never leave you, but it's also tied to you *and* to Shonlin. If you're ever compromised, Shonlin will be weakened."

"You mean, if I ever betray Shonlin?"

He shook his head. "No—the sphere will sense betrayal and return to me. As it hasn't returned to a future version of myself, I know you won't do that. What I mean is that if you're ill, magically, Shonlin will be ill. The sphere draws on its carrier's powers. When you're compromised, so is Shonlin because the sphere is a bridge between it and you. So, take care of yourself—keep your magic strong, keep your body strong. And do not allow yourself to become compromised."

CHAPTER EIGHT

ಐ ✦ ಡಿ

As Nicole left the meadow, her mind reeled with the final words Onyev had spoken. She vowed to herself not to let him down—as much as it was in her power.

The moment she stepped out of the forest, the scenery around her disappeared, and she was suddenly back with Austin in the bone dimension.

Nicole blinked, looking around. "How long was I gone?"

"A couple of hours," Austin said from where he leaned against the building's wall, a Michael Crichton novel in hand.

He jumped to his feet and hugged her. She pressed her face into his neck, relaxing in his arms. She wanted to tell him about the sphere, but would that be appropriate? Onyev hadn't given instructions about letting other people know. Not wanting to hide it from him, and wanting to see better, Nicole turned in his arms until her back was against his chest. She rested her head on his shoulder, and once comfortable, she wondered how to call the sphere.

The moment she thought about it coming to her, the sphere appeared in her hand. "Wow, that's pretty cool," she said, lifting it.

"What's that?"

"It's called the Kona Sphere," Nicole said. "Onyev gave it to me as a gift for kicking Lasia out of Shonlin."

Austin straightened, turning her so he could see her face. "Wow, really? He *gave* it to you? I read all about it while hanging out in the castle's library back when you had your blood sucked out by that bird. I can't believe it's yours now. That's so awesome, Nicole."

For a moment, Nicole sensed a little bit of jealousy, but she knew it wouldn't stay around long. Austin was a good guy and wouldn't begrudge her. Besides, if they were getting married, he would have access to it too.

Speaking of getting married . . . Nicole put her arms around his neck and gave him a quick peck on the mouth. "Can we . . . go back to our earlier discussion?"

"Yes, please. So, do you want to marry me?"

A smile tickled Nicole's lips, but she tried to hide it. She wasn't successful. "Is this you officially asking?"

"Yes." He hesitated, and a stricken expression crossed his face. "But I don't have a ring yet."

Nicole chuckled. "I guess I can't marry you, then." She poked his stomach to show she was teasing, then said, "If it makes you feel better, we can 'officialize' it once I have the ring, but yes, I *definitely* want to marry you."

A slow smile started across Austin's face, growing deeper, and the joy that entered his eyes made Nicole

WITHHOLD

squeeze him tighter.

"Awesome," he said. "When? Where?"

Nicole's heart started beating fast. She was getting married! "When—as soon as possible, of course. Before Keitus takes over everything. And as to where, I've always wanted to get married in a chapel." She hesitated. "What do you think is going to happen now that we know we can't stop Helen?"

Austin rubbed his face. "I don't know—no one knows."

"We'll have to approach the Great Ones." Even the thought of it made Nicole's knees weak and her stomach upset. But she saw no other alternative.

Austin shook his head, a frown appearing between his eyebrows. "No, we won't. Absolutely not. There has to be another way." He got even more agitated as he continued, "I'm not letting you near them, Nicole. Don't you remember what they said last time?"

Nicole put a finger to his lips. "We'll explore every avenue, I promise."

Even as she said the words, she knew she couldn't fully believe them. They didn't have time to "explore every avenue." And something told her she *would* be approaching the Great Ones—her gut instinct, which Onyev had told her to listen to and trust.

She needed to distract Austin. "When do you want to get married?"

Austin glanced away, worrying the inside of his cheek, a troubled expression on his face. Finally, he looked back at her. The worry lines had disappeared as he'd turned his thoughts to her question. "This weekend."

Nicole gasped. "Are you serious? How could we possibly pull it off so quickly?"

Austin took her hands. "We don't need something big."

She opened her mouth to respond, then closed it. She'd always wanted a big wedding. But there was quite a bit of merit to getting it finished as soon as possible, especially with the possible destruction of the world hanging over them. "Well, first let's see who can come. I want my brothers there. And Lizzie's family—definitely Lizzie's family." She paused, feeling a bit of sadness as she thought about her friends. It wasn't a very big list. "And Jacob's family and the Coolidges... Honestly, there aren't many I'd invite, but I do want to have the people I love there."

Austin agreed. "How about this—we tentatively set the wedding for this weekend, and if the majority can't come, we give them alternative days to choose from. Are you okay with that?"

Nicole kissed him on the cheek, fingering the hair at the nape of his neck. "That sounds great." Her heart fluttered as she thought about it again. She was getting married to Austin!

The door opened, and Jacob stepped out. "Are you guys done talking yet?" he asked with a twinkle in his eye. He raised his hands defensively. "Don't worry—I didn't listen to what you were saying. At least, I tried not to."

Austin and Nicole both nodded. "Yes, we're done," Austin said.

Jacob turned to her. "Nicole, I'm glad to see you back. And just in time—my dad and Azuriah want you to go

WITHHOLD

to Shonlin to see where the talismans are now so we can know where Keitus is." He hesitated. "Oh, and I get to be the first to congratulate you. I'm sure my parents will definitely want to attend your wedding this weekend."

Nicole and Austin thanked him, chuckling.

"So much for not listening to what we were talking about," Austin said, still laughing.

Nicole gave Austin a quick kiss before grabbing Jacob's hand so he could take her to the past and then to Shonlin in the present time. After a few flashes of light, they appeared in the library.

She knew she was safe—there weren't any more Shonlin traitors to surprise attack her—but still, her body wasn't quite ready to believe what her mind knew. Her stomach hurt, her hands began sweating, and a faint headache pulsed behind her left ear.

Pushing these new symptoms—and the old ones from her last visit here—aside, she ran up the stairs. This would be her first real experience with Shonlin in a very long time. The first few times she'd come, she hadn't completely known how to "operate" the forest. Soon after she'd learned what to do, she'd been attacked by Lasia.

Nicole couldn't wait to have a truly positive and fully enlightening experience.

She walked into the fifth-floor room and waved at the current guardian. His eyes were closed and he didn't respond, but Nicole didn't expect him to. She picked up the lantern and entered Shonlin. She sensed the hundreds of eyes that filled the forest on her. Waves of positive feelings cascaded over her in the form of their gratitude and pleasure at seeing her. Her heart and cheeks warmed, and she gave a little wave to acknowledge their thanks.

Nicole concentrated on the talismans, and several glowing orbs appeared in the forest about fifteen to twenty feet in front of her. She approached cautiously, not forgetting the last time she'd done this.

The moment Nicole raised her hand to the closest circle, visions entered her mind. She saw Keitus with several people near a table that had been set up in a forest. He had all four talismans and a skeleton out on the table. A spirit—Nicole frowned. It was Helen—hovered nearby. Keitus was doing something with the talismans, fumbling with them and the amulet Nicole had tried to prevent him from creating. He seemed a little frustrated.

Helen was eager, excited. Her hands visibly shook with anticipation, and the radiance and happiness that emanated not only from her face but her entire body made Nicole's eyes tear up. The poor woman had been through so much.

The minions that surrounded them were equally eager, but obviously for different reasons. Their lord and master was about to become far more powerful than anything they had ever served before. Nicole shook her head in disgust. It never ceased to amaze her how low desperate people would stoop.

Keitus, finally happy with what he'd been doing, looked up at Helen. "I'm ready." In his fist now was one magical item—the talismans had accepted the amulet, and they lined up seamlessly.

Helen nodded and said, "I grant you permission to inhabit my body. Take it—it's yours. I grant you permission to inhabit my body. Take it—it's yours." She

WITHHOLD

continued mumbling those words and a few others Nicole didn't understand over and over again.

Keitus put on the talisman like a necklace, then picked up the skeleton. He also began mumbling a chant that Nicole couldn't understand at all.

She had to stop them! Could she do something from here? She tried reaching through the link, but couldn't get past the orb. It filled her mind and blocked her vision every time she tried.

Nicole froze, watching as Keitus and the skeleton began glowing. Swirling winds blew around them. The trees and underbrush also started glowing, then exploded, the wind snatching the hurtling pieces from the air, spinning them around Keitus and the skeleton in his arms.

And then Keitus disappeared.

The skeleton he'd been holding disappeared a split second later. Everything, including the leaves, dirt, rocks and wood converged on that one point where Keitus had been. A body, a mass—something—formed in the middle of the whirlwind.

Nicole had expected a man like Keitus or a woman like Helen. What she hadn't expected was something not even human.

The thing that was forming was swollen, bulbous, and disgusting. Pus and blood leaked from multiple cracks on the thing's skin, visible through the whirlwind, which was now dying down. All of the objects and material that had been swirling in the wind were gone, having helped form the body. Nicole couldn't stop staring at it.

This thing, this creature that stood before Helen's spirit wasn't alive—it had to be dead. Had it formed correctly?

Was this how Keitus had envisioned himself once he'd achieved his desires? Was this what happened when the wrong body was united with the wrong spirit through magic?

The creature opened its mouth and screamed, "I am free!" Huge hands raised to a face that Nicole couldn't see. The beast explored those hands, turning them over. They were large and swollen, like the rest of the body. Warts lined the knuckles of fingers that were several inches around.

His hands were at least a foot wide each. The head was lumpy and not quite spherical. Grass and long, silvery hair sprouted from several places all over the head, back, and shoulders.

Nicole could tell when he started testing out his newfound powers. The table shook, raising several inches as Keitus laughed with glee.

Helen's spirit watched on, growing increasingly agitated and excited. Once Keitus seemed to be done playing, she stepped closer to him. "Please, where is my love?"

Keitus ignored her. He grabbed his knapsack and tried to sling it over his shoulder, but he was way too large. Instead, he thrust his arm through the shoulder straps and carried it somewhat like a purse.

Helen persisted. "You promised. I gave you my body. Where is Sutherland?"

Keitus still ignored her. With a flick of his hand, the table warped and twisted, then disappeared. He laughed. "My powers are unbelievable."

Helen became frantic. "Sutherland? Sutherland?

WITHHOLD

Where is he? You promised!"

Keitus turned and looked at her in annoyance. "Be gone, woman."

Anger crossed Helen's face, but before she could do anything, she froze, then exploded into a million pieces.

Keitus stared at the location where Helen had been, a grin on his cracked and bleeding lips. "Do not worry, my dear," he said. "You won't have need of your lover where you are now." He cackled. "And thanks for your body, you pathetic thing."

He paused, as if sensing something for the first time, then looked directly at Nicole. He waggled his index finger and tsked several times. "You have been a very bad girl, Nicole."

Nicole felt as Keitus tried to come through the link that connected her to the talismans, but was unable. The magic of Shonlin wouldn't let him.

Enraged, Keitus's body pulsed magic. It swelled around him, swirling and growing in strength. With a sudden roar, he directed that magic burst at Nicole.

She scrambled away, trying to close the connection between the two of them, but wasn't fast enough. The pulse flooded into the forest, slamming into her body and face. She fell to the ground, sensing as the magic flowed through her limbs and into her mind. A sudden sharp headache made her scream, and her vision blackened.

CHAPTER NINE

☙ ✦ ❧

When Nicole came to, she knew she was alone in the forest. Everything was quiet around her. She opened her eyes, but couldn't see anything. Her hands rushed to her face, exploring the shapes and angles, but nothing felt wrong or even hurt. Why couldn't she see?

She whimpered, getting to her knees and feeling around the forest floor. Her hands bumped into the lantern, and she picked it up, clenching it tightly. Grateful that her internal compass was still working, she started inching across the forest floor, using one hand to monitor the ground and the other to protect her face while holding the lantern.

The going was slow, and it was easy to get discouraged. Would she—*could* she—reach the door on her own? She couldn't even see where it was, and experience told her this forest was never-ending.

WITHHOLD

Getting lost was very likely. She needed help.

Nicole pressed through her mental connection to the current guardian, seeking his attention, hoping he was there. She nearly sobbed when she recognized his presence.

"Nicole?" he said. "The door is open. I'm standing by it."

"I can hear you," Nicole said. "Please keep talking."

The guardian did so, describing the things around her. Following his voice, she continued through the forest, passing large tree trunks and making it through thick underbrush. It was slow and painful, and by the end, her arms and hands had been pricked so many times, she was sure they were bleeding everywhere.

She couldn't help but feel bitter that yet again, her experience in Shonlin had ended up being a negative one. How many of the other guardians had horrible things happen when they visited the place? Probably not a lot. It was ridiculous.

Nicole finally reached the library, sensing as the guardian moved out of the way to make room for her. Once sure she'd cleared the doorway, she set down the lantern and heard the wall shut behind her. Then she got to her feet, knowing that walking would be easier than crawling. Her hands and knees needed a break.

"Thanks for your help," she said to the guardian.

He didn't respond. With one hand on the wall and the other in front of her, she made her way through the room, going slowly and hesitatingly. It took what felt like ten minutes to reach the door that led to the rest of the library.

She found the knob and pushed the door open, then stumbled over the threshold. "Jacob?"

Someone scrambled to their feet nearby. "Holy cow, Nicole."

She raised her hands to her face. "Is it that bad?"

Jacob touched her shoulder. "You're pretty scratched up. What happened?"

"Keitus saw me watching and attacked. He's got what he wants. The talismans, Helen's body, *his* new body." She started trembling. "It's awful. He's so powerful! He was able to push his magic through the link to me—I didn't even know that was possible."

Jacob grabbed her arm, squeezing a little too tightly as he started freaking out too. "Oh, no. Oh, no," he said. "What should we do?"

"We have to heal me. I can't go anywhere until I can see."

"Are you completely blind? Because . . . I don't want to be a jerk, but it's magically inflicted, and who knows how long it'll take to heal. Nicole, I have to get back to my family to warn them. We have to warn everyone!"

"Do you have your Minya?"

Nicole heard Jacob searching his bag. "Not with me, no," Jacob said. "She went out for honey yesterday and I haven't seen her since. I can call her, but if she's not nearby, she won't hear it."

Nicole grumbled, trying to resist the urge to lash out at him for letting his Minya leave. He couldn't have known this would happen. "We're in a hurry, I know, but it'll take me much longer to walk to the door in this condition than if I slept, healed, and we ran." She paused, thinking, and almost didn't continue, but wanted to make sure everything was out in the open. "On the other hand, we need to consider what will happen if I still can't see when I wake up. I won't be able to find my way out of this place, and we'll have lost the time we took to heal me." She tried to keep the tremble out of her voice. "I don't know what to do."

She heard as Jacob took a deep breath and released it. "Okay. We'll heal you first—Kaede sap is powerful. It'll fix your eyes. While you're sleeping, I'll call Early."

Nicole nodded, just as frustrated at being forced to take a break. Splitting up wasn't an option—they needed each other for protection.

Jacob applied the salve to her eyes, and Nicole settled on the marble floor of the library to sleep.

What felt like only moments later, she awoke. She gingerly touched her eyes, hesitating. But when she opened her eyes, she could see. Yay! She jerked to a sitting position. "Jacob?"

He scrambled into view from where he had been leaning against the railing. "You're awake already?"

"And I can see!"

"Oh, good," Jacob said with relief. "You only slept for an hour. Let's go." He jumped to his feet and rushed to help her up. "How do you feel?"

"Great. Like it never happened."

They ran down the steps and dashed across the floor of the library. Just as they were about to pull the doors open, Nicole gasped, stumbling, stopping. Everything *wasn't* okay. She couldn't sense her magic. She couldn't sense *anything* magical. Nothing pulsed around her, and no sign of any elemental control resonated within her. Her reserves that were usually walled up in a vast ocean were gone too. "Jacob, I can't sense my magic. It's gone. It's completely gone!"

He dragged a hand down his face. "We'll have to tackle that when we get to the castle."

She nodded, struggling to keep the tears from falling. He was right—there were bigger things to worry about. But what had Keitus done to her?

Jacob burst through the doors, then stopped, his mouth hanging open as he stared at the sky. Nicole joined him and looked up too. Dark green clouds were forming quickly, blocking the sun, casting a green haze over everything.

"Keitus?" Nicole asked.

Jacob's face set in a grimace. "Yes. I've seen this before. It's not good. We have to go. *Now.*"

Without hesitation, they barreled down the steps and into the streets, dashing through the ruins of Edana.

They were nearing the door Jacob usually used when screams and roars began filling the air, creatures shifting into the forest on either side of them.

Nicole knew without having to look that these beings were enemies, servants of Keitus. She and Jacob met eyes, then both put on a burst of speed. The door was in view when Jacob started fumbling at his pocket, pulling out the key. He thrust it into the lock, muttering, then flinging the door open.

Magical pulses hammered into Nicole from behind.

WITHHOLD

She was grateful to sense them—grateful to sense *anything* magical—but her heart ached, wishing she could turn and attack.

Jacob slammed the door shut behind them, and they entered a very full throne room. King Dmitri and Queen Arien were waiting for them, along with what looked like hundreds of people. Nicole turned, watching as guards rushed the door and held it shut. Loud banging sounded from the other side.

Nicole glanced at the king and queen. "What's going on?"

"The castle's under attack," Dmitri said.

Jacob dragged his hand through his hair. "Bad news. Keitus got what he needed. He's attacking—he's the one doing this."

"We were afraid of that," the queen said. "We waited for you as long as we could, gathering as many people as possible." She put her face in her hands. "So many have died already."

This was the first time Nicole had ever seen Arien not completely composed. She and Jacob looked at each other.

"We have to get out of here," Nicole said. "No telling how many servants Keitus has by now."

As if in response, the door began splintering. The guards weren't holding it well enough—they couldn't. There were too few of them.

The air outside the castle was thick and very green, making it impossible to see far. Even without the sun, Nicole still sensed the darkness approaching. Screams filtered through the door, and her heart broke for the innocent who hadn't reached the throne room in time.

Jacob rushed to a door on the opposite side of the room. He created a link and held it open. "She's right. Come on, everyone, inside my house back on earth. Let's go. Hurry!"

The room quickly emptied, and Nicole watched as Jacob's family, Azuriah, a bunch of guards, Aldo, servants, and a few creatures she didn't recognize flooded through Jacob's link. "Where's the Fat Lady?" Nicole asked while Dmitri spoke with the guards holding the door.

Aldo shook his head. "She's in the hallway. We tried to get her in, but she was already surrounded by villains when the door got flooded." He motioned to the dead bodies that littered the floor. "They got through before she told us to leave her."

Nicole could hear the pain in Aldo's voice—he and the Fat Lady were good friends. She prayed the woman was okay.

She watched as more innocent people escaped through Jacob's link and she almost started crying. She could tell from the expression on Jacob's face that he was feeling the same. Even though a lot of things had happened to help Keitus rise to success, what it all boiled down to was that she and Jacob had failed in their duties. Resolve bubbled up inside her. She *would* put an end to this.

Dmitri joined his family, making sure they were all through the link. He motioned for Nicole to go too, then turned and yelled, "Come now!"

The guards looked back at him with some

WITHHOLD

hesitation—they didn't want to put their king in danger by leaving the door unguarded, Nicole suspected.

"Hurry!" Dmitri said.

They didn't need any more urging. As one, they released their hold on the doors and sprang across the stone floor.

CHAPTER TEN

Banging sounded before everything quieted for a moment. Then creatures burst through the doors, flowing into the room—humans, monsters, beings of all shapes and sizes, each carrying weapons and shod with armor.

The guards, Dmitri, and Nicole stepped through the link into what looked like the living room of a traditional American home just as the monsters reached that side of the room. Jacob slammed the door, but it shut on something and popped back open.

A large monster with warts on his face forced his way through, and in that brief moment when the door was open again, Nicole saw the Fat Lady running across the throne room, surrounded by monsters who were charging the link. Jacob shut the door again, this time successfully.

WITHHOLD

"We have to get her!" Nicole shouted, but her voice was drowned by the noise of the guards who were fighting the monster.

The beast wielded a huge axe and swung it at everyone nearby, and there were a *lot* of people within reach. The living room of what looked like a traditional American home was small, and though most of the people had moved on to other rooms, many were straining to see what was going on. Guards had their swords out and were fighting the creature off, but the thing was fast and strong.

A deafening boom sounded through the air, and Nicole's hands covered her ears reflexively. Dmitri stood near the front door holding a rifle. The beast growled at him before hefting the axe and charging. Another boom thundered through the room. Then another, and another, each one punctuated with the sound of casings hitting the wooden floor.

Finally, the creature dropped dead. Nicole slumped against the nearest wall, her knees shaking, her heart beating so fast, she felt like she would pass out. In the silence, she could hear sniffling and gasping.

She gathered her strength, forced herself away from the wall, and stepped around the monster to join Dmitri, who was peering outside. Nicole also glanced out the window. The sky was clear here, thankfully.

"How much time do you think we have before Keitus attacks earth?" she asked.

"Not much," Dmitri said.

He grabbed a box of bullets and a leather knapsack from a shelf behind the front door before shoving the bullets in the knapsack and turning to his son. "We need to go on the offensive." He glanced around the room. "Some of you are my best fighters. I need you to stay here, near the link to the Makalo village, and guard it, making sure nobody comes through." He pinched the bridge of his nose before saying, "The rest of us will head to Nicole's dimension of earth to gather as many Aretes as possible to fight Keitus."

Nicole bit her lip. "Will the Fat Lady be okay?"

Arien put a hand to her neck and looked at the ceiling, blinking tears out of her eyes. "I hope so. She's smart. She should be okay."

Dmitri put his arm around his wife. "She'll be fine."

"I saw her running for the door. She needs our help." Her heart ached again when she remembered the expression of hope and despair on the Fat Lady's face. *Please, please be okay.*

Arien paled, her hand still at her neck. She looked at her husband. "Can we get her?"

Dmitri shook his head, his mouth in a thin line. "We can't take on all of the monsters in that room—you saw how hard it was to stop this one. We'll get her as soon as we have more help."

Nicole gasped, looking around the room. "Where's Austin?" The last time she'd seen him had been in the bone dimension when Jacob opened the door and they'd gone to Shonlin. "And Lizzie?"

"Austin's probably at Coolidge's house," Jacob said. "I left the link there open before taking you to Shonlin. And Lizzie is probably still at school—that's where she said she was heading."

WITHHOLD

Nicole put a hand over her heart and drew in a deep breath. She hoped they were safe. "Now what?"

Dmitri motioned to Jacob. "Create a link to Mr. Coolidge's house."

"In which dimension?" Jacob asked. "His or ours?"

"His. We'll start gathering people there—specifically magical ones—to fight Keitus."

Before they left, Dmitri sent a message to the Makalos, letting them know what was going on and asking how they were doing in the village. Akeno's dad responded immediately. He said they were holing up, that they'd be safe and had been safe through similar circumstances before.

Jacob took them to Coolidge's house. This dimension of earth hadn't been touched yet either—the sky was still bright and clear. Nicole knew that Keitus would attack eventually. She just hoped they would be more prepared.

She stepped through the door into Coolidge's front room and started crying in relief when she saw Austin on the couch. He immediately jumped to his feet, rushed across the room, and threw his arms around her. "What's the matter?"

Nicole sniffled. "I watched Keitus come to power. He went after Jacob's world. The Fat Lady got trapped and left behind, and we barely made it out in time. He'll be coming here soon." A thought flitted through her mind. How would she and Austin get married now? She knew it was trivial, but still, Keitus had stolen so much from her over the past few months, and stealing this from her was just too much.

"I'm sorry I wasn't there," Austin said.

Dmitri put a hand on his shoulder. "There isn't anything you could have done to stop it."

Austin nodded and held Nicole tighter, rubbing her back.

Jacob sat on the couch, putting his head in his hands. "I'm going to Time-See—figure out what's going on."

Nicole and the others alternated pacing and waiting on one of the couches or armchairs. Coolidge and Hayla joined them, and Nicole filled them in on what had happened. She couldn't help but check the skies every couple of seconds. So far, they remained clear.

After five minutes, Jacob looked up. "Keitus has all of my world now. The Fat Lady is still alive. The Makalos are fine—having all of their magic again is really helping them, and they've been able to seal off their village."

"What are Keitus's forces doing with the people?" Dmitri asked.

"They're fighting and killing anyone who resists, and accepting volunteers for their army. Those who don't fight or volunteer are frozen in place. That's what happened to the Fat Lady."

"Frozen?" Arien asked.

Jacob nodded. "But not like ice. They turn green and the air leaves their bodies."

"How do you know they're still alive?" Hayla asked, her hands resting on her stomach.

Nicole's heart went out to the woman—she couldn't imagine what it would be like to face this sort of trial while pregnant.

"Because I can see it in their eyes," Jacob said. "The monsters are searching through those who are frozen and selecting big, strong fighters. They unfreeze them and try to get them to join Keitus." His eyes narrowed. "They're murdering anyone who doesn't help."

"What's Keitus going to do?" Nicole asked. "I mean, he's already got everything he wants, right?"

Coolidge shook his head. "What would *anyone* do with massive amounts of power and wealth? Amass more and more of it. There's no end to the reach he'll have, and who knows how many inhabited planets are in the universe that he can take over."

Nicole nodded. "I know, but eventually, he'll have everything. What I want to know is what happens then, when there isn't anything left to conquer?"

Coolidge ran his hands down his face. "He'll have to fight to maintain that hold. It's not going to be easy for him."

"But with all the power he has . . ." Jacob said. "I mean, he rivals the Great Ones now."

Nicole felt like crying again. "Power . . . I still can't sense my powers." She turned to Jacob. "They haven't come back yet!"

She sank to the couch as she remembered what Onyev had said about Shonlin. Had Keitus discovered the weakness yet? While Nicole was compromised magically, and she definitely would consider this being compromised, Shonlin would be weakened, surely granting Keitus access. He was too powerful now for a weakened Shonlin to withstand any sort of attack. She had to do something about this!

"Wait. What's going on?" Coolidge asked.

Nicole quickly updated him on what happened in the

forest.

He shook his head. "This is not good. He took your magic."

"Keitus was very mad at me. Why didn't he just kill me?"

No one responded. Probably because no one knew the answer.

Queen Arien gave a little shriek, staring out the window. "Clouds!" she said, motioning frantically.

CHAPTER ELEVEN

☙ ♦ ❧

Everyone rushed to join her, and Nicole was dismayed to see the sky filling with thunderheads that had a greenish tinge to them. Coolidge's phone started dinging repeatedly, and Austin's rang. He answered it, put it on speakerphone, and set it on the table in the middle of the room.

"Dad, you okay?" he said.

"Good, you're safe," Dave said. "Yes, we're fine, but your mother and I were worried. Huge amounts of magic are trying to break into our place. Is that going on in Seattle?"

Austin shook his head, glancing out the window. "No, not here. How long since that started?"

"About five minutes ago. We wondered if it was something special for us, then realized it might be connected to Keitus."

Nicole bit her lip. Why had Keitus attacked Austin's

parents place first? Yes, they were more powerful. But wouldn't Keitus have been drawn to a place where more magic was gathered? Like the university?

She turned to Jacob, grabbing him. "We have to get Lizzie. Now. I don't care what she's doing. We have to bring her back."

Jacob nodded. His eyes glazed over for a moment, then he returned and said, "She's in English class. Let's get her."

Coolidge jumped to his feet. "I'm coming too. We have to warn the university."

Jacob opened a link to Lizzie's classroom. They barged through the door, rushing into the room, interrupting the discussion. The teacher was annoyed at first until she saw Coolidge.

"What's going on?" she asked him.

"Things that aren't good." He turned to the classroom. "Pack your stuff and go. Earth is about be taken over by an evil and very powerful being. You have minutes, maybe less, to get somewhere relatively safe."

Lizzie joined Nicole up front as people began jumping over chairs and desks to get out of class. Everyone recognized Nicole and her group. She ignored the stares they received from students as they rushed past.

Coolidge turned to Jacob. "Take us to the university president's office."

Jacob nodded, the key still in hand. He created a link and opened the door. Coolidge didn't wait for anyone else before striding through. "Get in touch with the president of the United States—someone with more authority than us. Tell him earth is about to be attacked."

WITHHOLD

The university president, Professor Garcia, stared at Coolidge in shock. "What are you talking about?"

Nicole's heart sank in dismay. They hadn't passed along a warning in a very long time—not since their initial meeting with Professor Smith months and months ago. She'd never once believed it would come to this. How much time would they lose over people not believing or being caught off guard?

Coolidge didn't have time to explain. At that moment, a huge magical pulse swept through the room, slamming into everyone. Screams echoed in the hallway. Professor Garcia opened a drawer and pulled out a cell phone. He pushed a single button and placed the phone on the middle of his desk, turning on it to speakerphone.

"Payne here," a man said.

"Give the phone to the president."

There was some shuffling in the background, then someone said, "Yes?"

It was a curt, abrupt voice, and Nicole recognized it immediately.

"You might want to listen to this." Garcia nodded at Coolidge.

Coolidge placed both hands on the desk, leaning over the phone. "I don't have much time, Mr. President. You need to get a message out to as many people and countries as you can. Earth is about to be attacked by an immortal being named Keitus. He is powerful—rivaling even the Great Ones who visited last year."

Nicole heard what sounded like the snapping of fingers, then the president said, "How will the attacks come?"

Coolidge glanced at Nicole and Jacob.

"They've already begun," Jacob said, his voice deeper than usual with the intensity of the situation.

"Watch the skies," Nicole said. "The sun will be covered first."

"With greenish clouds?"

"Yes."

"It's already begun here. What can we expect from this attack?"

"Demons, and lots of them," Nicole said. "They'll kill or freeze those who oppose them, and recruit any who want to help."

The president cursed. "Why weren't we warn—"

The call was dropped.

No one said anything. Nicole's mouth went dry. She thought they would have more time than this.

Garcia turned on the TV and began flipping through channels. Reporters were freaking out. Some stations were completely gone, and others were full of confused people who weren't sure what was happening. One station had been reporting on another event when demons began attacking there, so they had first-hand footage and were playing it over and over again. Those videos showed people scrambling, running, and screaming.

"How do we stop this?" Garcia asked. Then he shook his head and raised his hand, stopping any responses from coming. "Coolidge, this is your area. I'll grant you access to all of the university resources and any equipment or funds you might need. But I *must* take care of my teachers and students."

Nicole saw the wisdom in that. He had to start with

his stewardship before worrying about the rest of the world.

"What's our game plan?" she asked as she and the others rushed through Jacob's link back to Coolidge's house. She'd considered bringing up Shonlin, but couldn't do it. Who knew what sort powers Keitus had? The chances that he could hear any and all conversations were high. There was no way she'd put Shonlin in that much jeopardy. She so wished they'd had more time to plan for this.

"We need your magic back," Coolidge said.

Relief rushed over her. She hated that Shonlin was weak while she didn't have her powers, and it really was imperative that they get things figured out as soon as possible, but she hated not being able to explain this to the others. "I definitely agree that it should be on our list, but why is it the *first* thing you bring up?"

"We need your help," he said. "You're more powerful than the vast majority of Aretes out there, and we lost a lot of our Silvers last year when the Great Ones came."

Nicole only nodded in response. With her luck, *if* there was a resolution, it would be a long and painful one. She sensed the sphere in her pocket, ready for her to use at any moment. How was Shonlin doing now?

"Jacob, take me to Onyev," Nicole said. "I'm not sure he'll be able to help, but I hope he can."

"Okay, but before we go," Jacob said, "let me check and see how everything is going."

Nicole agreed and sat on the couch to wait. It didn't take long. Jacob returned, his expression grave. "The Fire Pulser's world has surrendered. Renforth's too. And here, Aretes are losing—there aren't enough of them. All of Europe is enslaved now, and Africa and Asia look to be following soon."

He looked up at Nicole and their friends. "It's really, really bad out there."

CHAPTER TWELVE

ଛ ♦ ଓ

Nicole felt tears prickle the backs of her eyes. How could they possibly win this battle? She knew Europe didn't have many Aretes to begin with, but things were going faster than she'd expected.

Austin gave Nicole a quick kiss, then Jacob took her hand. Everything flashed around them, and Nicole found herself outside Onyev's place.

Once she'd located him, Nicole explained what was going on.

He shook his head, his brow furrowed. "Things are turbulent for us here, but now they feel small in comparison to what you're going through." He paced, hands behind his back. "I'm glad you came to see me. I've sensed weakness in Shonlin over the past few hours, and now that you're here, I understand why."

"He stole my magic, and we don't know how to get it back. Or even if we can. And I didn't know what to tell my friends—I suspect that Keitus can hear our conversations. I couldn't talk about my connection to Shonlin and risk him gaining access to the knowledge there."

"I appreciate that." Onyev sighed. "Let's hope the loss of your magic isn't permanent. We'll find out soon enough."

He tapped his cheek, still pacing, a distant expression on his face. He began mumbling to himself, saying things Nicole didn't understand—possibly words in other languages. Finally, he turned to face Nicole.

"There is a potion that might work—the Dramocia. It consists mostly of metals. Metals are usually dangerous, but in this potion, they work to expel the toxins Keitus put inside you. Do you know someone who can help you get special ingredients? And we'll need a way to record them. I've never written them down."

He turned toward the door, presumably to call someone in to write the ingredients, but Nicole put up her hand and stopped him.

"I've got something here."

She pulled out her phone, glad she left it powered off through everything. The battery was still at eighty-percent.

Onyev dictated the ingredients as Nicole wrote. She had him spell out a couple of them. When she'd finished, she looked over the list. Four metals, three of which she vaguely remembered from her high school chemistry class.

Rhodium. Ruthenium. Osmium. Clarion.

"Does clarion come from Eklaron?" she asked.

WITHHOLD

"Yes," Onyev said. "It's incredibly rare."

Naturally.

"The only known mine is thousands of miles from here—on the other side of the planet."

Nicole got her feet and began pacing. "Do we just mix everything together?"

"Yes." Onyev lowered himself to the bench. He looked tired. "Find someone skilled in creating potions."

"I'm not sure where someone like that would be."

"Eklaron has many."

Nicole chewed her lip. "That'll be a problem. Keitus has taken over Eklaron already."

Onyev looked stricken. "Shonlin . . ." he whispered. "Do what you must, Nicole. You know the stakes."

She couldn't help but wonder why Onyev gave her the sphere if it was so imperative that it be kept safe. She was grateful he trusted her so much, though, and had a feeling the sphere would come in handy.

Nicole returned to Jacob and told him everything—the sphere, her theory about Keitus being able to hear them in the present time, and how her powers were tied to Shonlin.

"We have to get the Fat Lady," Jacob said once she'd finished. "She's the best potions master I know. Actually, she's the *only* one I know."

Nicole rubbed her eyes. "I was worried you'd say something like that. She's kind of stuck right now."

"Yeah." A troubled expression crossed Jacob's face. "And we can't rescue her without having a place to take her."

Nicole nodded. Where would that be? They wouldn't

have access to earth much longer, and only Nicole could enter Shonlin. Actually, all of Eklaron was off limits. She briefly thought about Renforth's planet, but as Jacob said, it had already been enslaved. What else was there?

"Oh, I know!" she said.

"What?"

"Anna Morse's dimension."

Jacob's face lit up. "Good idea. He hasn't touched it yet. Probably because he already pretty much owns it."

Excited to have a plan, they returned to the present time and their friends. Without telling anyone what was going on, Jacob opened a link from Coolidge's place to the bone dimension. He put a finger to his lips and then motioned for everyone to follow him through.

They set up camp in the place where Keitus had stayed for so long, where they found the core he'd used to prevent Jacob from spying on him. It was in a corner of the old abandoned cabin.

Austin chuckled. "How about we use his magic against him? Stop him from listening in on us?"

"If we can," Coolidge said. "It might not function for us."

Lizzie put her hands on her hips. "Even if we get it to work, if he thinks to look here, he'll stop us immediately. Don't forget he's got the talismans, which give him the power to weaken and reveal. Let's just hope he won't think about checking here at all because if he does, we're toast."

"We need to be constantly moving to prevent anything from happening," Coolidge said.

Everyone agreed to that.

WITHHOLD

Nicole leaned against the doorframe, facing her friends inside the cabin. "For reasons I can't explain, our biggest priority needs to be to rescue the Fat Lady."

"But how?" Austin asked.

"The same way you got the first talisman," Coolidge said. "Jacob puts up a bubble, and everyone sneaks around inside it while he uses his ability to see emotions and figure out where all of the 'bad guys' are."

Jacob held up a hand. "Seeing emotions only works if they belong to intelligent beings. Unintelligent beings can still be enemies, but I won't see their emotions."

"That's good to know," Coolidge said.

"So, I'm game," Austin said. "Who's going?"

CHAPTER THIRTEEN

After more debate, it was decided that Nicole, Azuriah, Austin, and Coolidge would form the team. Azuriah volunteered to take Jacob's spot. They'd need him to watch and open a link once they finished. If he was with them when they were attacked, he wouldn't be able to get them out. Instead, Azuriah would do the bubble thing.

Lizzie, Dmitri, Arien, and Aldo would stay behind and quietly scout out new campground spots.

Nicole gave her best friend a hug, holding her tightly. "Austin proposed to me," she whispered. "I said yes, and we were going to get married this weekend, then Keitus attacked and spoiled our plans."

Lizzie pulled back, hands on her friend's shoulders. "I'm so sorry," she whispered, her usual bounce and cheer gone. "Please, please be safe. I want to come to your wedding."

WITHHOLD

Nicole half smiled, her body tired, her mind exhausted. "Are you guys going to split up to search for camping spots or stick together?"

"I'm going with Aldo. He and I decided to look for places near where anything bad has happened to us—it was my idea. I figured those would be the last places Keitus would think to look."

Nicole hugged Lizzie again. "Genius idea. I'll be praying for you."

"Same."

Nicole joined the others and watched as Jacob pulled the key out of his pocket. He turned and asked if everyone was ready.

"Don't forget to watch each other closely," Coolidge said to those staying behind. "Remember that the Croents can take on the shape of loved ones."

"In case anything happens and you aren't able to regroup with us," Lizzie said, "what do we do once this is over?"

"Gather as many people together as possible to attack Keitus," Coolidge said.

Nicole shook her head, motioning at Jacob to stop in case he was about to open the link. "No—that's a bad idea. He's way too powerful. We have to communicate with the Great Ones. They're the only ones who can stop him."

Most disagreed with this plan, especially Austin, and they all started arguing with her. Only Lizzie and Jacob thought she might be right, but even they were doubtful. Azuriah didn't care what they did as long as it got them somewhere.

Nicole sighed to herself. She'd finish convincing Lizzie and Jacob later, but why did *Azuriah* not have a problem with it when traditionally, he disagreed with her simply because it was her?

Pushing her frustrations aside, Nicole nodded when Jacob asked if she was ready. He keyed them to the Fat Lady's cabin, then shut the door and Time-Saw to make sure it was clear out front. It was, and he popped the door open.

Nicole and the others followed him around back, past some clotheslines, and up into the forested hills behind the cabin. As they walked, Jacob whispered instructions. "The Fat Lady still has protections on her cabin," he said. "I'll hang out there and watch until you're ready to come back. Then I'll open a link to the door closest to you."

He showed them the entrance to a tunnel. "It'll take you into the castle. It runs beneath Maivoryl City and is long, dark, and very musty, but as far as we know, no one else is aware of it. Good luck. I'll be watching."

The tunnel was deserted and damp, just as Jacob said it would be. Nicole swore she heard something scampering past a few times, but even when she shone her flashlight down, she never saw anything.

After nearly an hour of walking, they finally reached the other side, where a set of cement stairs rose sharply. Azuriah led them up, then at the top, he Time-Saw to make sure the way was safe. Because he was able to see emotions as well, he would guide them to the Fat Lady.

The halls were deserted. Coolidge speculated that Keitus's demons had already conquered this part of the castle. Anyone who would have resisted had been frozen

WITHHOLD

or killed.

They found the Fat Lady in the throne room right where Nicole had last seen her. An expression of fear was on her face, one hand raised to defend herself, the other protecting her head.

"How do we unfreeze her?" Coolidge asked.

No one had an answer. There was no way they would be able to move her—she was too big. Why hadn't they thought of that before?

Nicole had an idea, and as if reading her mind, the sphere was suddenly in her hand in her pocket.

"I might be able to find something to help us," she whispered. "Azuriah, would you take us to a quiet room? I need a couple of minutes."

He did so, leading them through the dark halls and into a deserted corner room of the castle. Nicole took the sphere out of her pocket and held it level with her face, staring at it, ignoring the others. It didn't do anything. She gave it a little shake, then stared at it again. Still nothing. She wished she could send a wisp of magic to it, willing it to tell her what to do, but that obviously wouldn't work. What, then?

Finally, she imagined herself in Shonlin, holding the sphere tightly in her hand, asking it to grant her access. She gasped as the library opened into a vision before her, allowing her to see both her current surroundings in the castle *and* the fifth floor of the library. It was a little disorienting at first, but she pushed aside her confusion and approached the guardian. His eyes were open, as they usually were when she saw him like this. He smiled and opened the door for her.

Nicole stepped forward, but hesitated. He might know what she needed. She turned to him. "I need a way to help someone magically frozen be able to move again."

He thought for a moment, then looked at the book that was always near the door under protective glass. He removed the glass box. Opening the book, he trailed his finger down the pages one after the other.

The guardian nodded. "This isn't a perfect match, but it's the only thing within Shonlin's borders that'll help."

He guided her to the appropriate shelf. Nicole repeated the words that rushed into her mind, unsealing a walking stick. The stick glowed momentarily and she picked it up, glancing at the guardian.

"What does it do?"

"Increases the speed of the user. It will enable your friend to move. Use caution—it might not be fast enough." He took a deep breath. "And please hurry, Nicole. I can sense the darkness pressing in again. We need your strength as soon as possible."

Nicole thanked him and left the room. Just as the door closed behind her, the vision ended and she could only see the dark interior of the castle. The walking stick was now in her hand. She stared at it, marveling at the power the sphere gave her.

"That's quite some magical item you have," Azuriah said.

"Do you mean the sphere or the walking stick?" she asked.

"Potentially both. Mostly the sphere."

He led the way back to the Fat Lady, and Nicole

WITHHOLD

placed the walking stick in her hand. The woman's fingers slowly, slowly curled around it. Once it was fully in her grasp, she inched her head up and looked into the faces of her friends.

"You've . . . come . . . for . . . me," she said.

Nicole and the others looked at each other. If this was the fastest the Fat Lady could go, they'd never get her out before somebody caught them.

"The curse is still on her," Coolidge said.

"The guardian said this is the only thing that would help," Nicole said. "I don't know if it's possible to remove the curse completely."

The Fat Lady started for the throne room door, using the walking stick to support herself, guided by Azuriah. The more she used the stick, the faster she went, but it still wasn't enough.

Streams of magic started pricking Nicole in the back, and she whirled toward the door. Nothing was there.

"We've got company headed this way!" Azuriah shrieked.

CHAPTER FOURTEEN

☙ ♦ ❧

Nicole and the others surrounded the Fat Lady while Azuriah put up his bubble. They were nearly to the door of the throne room when a demon appeared. Like the first demon they'd fought that day, this one had an axe. He lifted it, letting it drop toward Coolidge's head, the person nearest him. The axe bounced off Azuriah's bubble, and Nicole breathed a sigh of relief. She'd forgotten it was basically an invisible shield.

Coolidge's magic swirled around him, also invisible to the demon, and fire exploded on the creature, burning it to a crisp. It dropped to the ground, breaking into chunks.

"Good . . . trick . . .," the Fat Lady said.

He nodded. "Let's keep going. I won't be able to do that very often."

More demons entered the room. They were able

see through the bubble, but their war cries and grunts of anger were muffled. Austin and Coolidge fought with magic. Nicole could sense their powers, but still couldn't feel her own. She absolutely hated feeling so useless.

Now that she had found a magical item for the Fat Lady to use, she was only a hindrance. What could she do to help?

Nicole cringed when both Coolidge and Austin's powers started waning. Azuriah was tiring as well. They were still too far from the door, and even if Jacob opened a link for them now, that distance could take several minutes to cross. The Fat Lady was creeping along. Nicole wrung her hands, doing her best not to distract the others. She had to do something!

She pulled the sphere from her pocket, unsure what to do with it, but realizing if she didn't do something, they'd end up dead. She imagined herself in Shonlin again and approached the guardian.

"What are you in need of?"

"A weapon—something to fight against magic."

"Close or long range?"

Nicole hesitated, thinking. "Not really close, but within ten feet."

The guardian again went to the book, flipping through the pages. He murmured to himself as he searched. Several times, he chose something only to change his mind. Nicole resisted the urge to hurry him. Finally, he led her to a shelf. The magical item Nicole unsealed was an umbrella.

Was he serious? "What will it do?"

"Open it and you'll find out. But don't point it toward

a friend."

Nicole thanked him, left, and the vision closed. Once she had her bearings, she gasped, seeing that she and her friends were surrounded by demons. There were *tons* of them now! She pointed the umbrella toward the nearest one and opened and closed it several times.

At first, nothing happened. Then the demon began to melt. Nicole wasn't sure why. Was the umbrella spreading an invisible acid or poison?

Azuriah's bubble started wavering.

Her curiosity replaced with determination, Nicole used the umbrella to blaze a way through the monsters, then turned to watch the Fat Lady follow slowly. Just as they arrived at their destination, Azuriah's bubble died. The door popped open and Jacob jumped out, replacing Azuriah's shield with one of his own.

"Hurry, hurry!" he said, waving everyone through.

Nicole stayed behind the Fat Lady as Azuriah, Coolidge, and Austin urged her onward. The woman's steps had begun to slow as she tired from fighting the curse. Nicole continued using the umbrella, watching as monster after monster dropped, melting like wax.

Finally, the Fat Lady cleared the doorway, and Nicole jumped through, into the Fat Lady's cabin. Jacob closed the link behind them.

The Fat Lady turned to Nicole, walking stick still in hand, a cranky expression on her face. "I assume . . . the reason . . . you got me . . . is because you need something."

Nicole knitted her eyebrows, understanding the real question behind what the woman was saying. It was

WITHHOLD

something to the effect of, "There'd better be a good reason for you risking yourselves to save me or you're huge idiots."

"We need you to make something called the Dramocia potion," Nicole said.

"I know . . . of it. Don't remember . . . what the ingredients are. Do you have them . . . already?"

"No, none of them."

"Tell me . . . what you need."

Nicole repeated the names of the metals, happy to see the Fat Lady nod and start toward her shelf. Apparently, she had two of them, and the castle had the others.

While the Fat Lady searched for the two she had, Jacob keyed back to Aldo's lab in the castle. He got in and out quickly—that section of the castle was deserted—then handed over the ingredients.

The Fat Lady got started on it immediately. Nicole really hated that it took so long for the poor woman to move around. But even so, she was able to mix everything in only an hour. While waiting, Nicole looked at the ring Austin had given her a while ago—the one that let them direct positive thoughts to each other. She switched it from her right hand, putting it on her left ring finger. It was too big, but it felt right there, now that they were engaged. She needed something to occupy her mind.

Austin watched her playing with the ring and sent her a smile, giving her knee a gentle squeeze. Such a small action on his part warmed her heart considerably. How she hoped they'd get through this ordeal quickly and as painlessly as possible!

While waiting, Jacob watched and relayed

information to them as more and more of earth was enslaved. Nicole tried not to dwell on it—especially when she remembered Lizzie's family. Please be okay!

After another twenty minutes, the Fat Lady announced that the potion was done.

"Do you know . . . how you need to take it?" the Fat Lady asked. "I know it has special requirements."

Nicole frowned. That was definitely something she should have asked. "I'm not sure. Onyev didn't say anything."

"Well, you'd better . . . go find out."

Though Nicole agreed with the Fat Lady, she still groaned inwardly at yet another delay. She closed her eyes and took a deep breath, then allowed Jacob to take her back to Gratitude.

The patriarch wasn't surprised to see her. "You must have found a potions master."

"I did. She got everything mixed together, and now I need to know how to take it."

He nodded. "Mix it with water—one gram of potion for each teaspoon. You'll take it one spoonful at a time, repeated every hour, until the potion is gone." He looked her directly in the eye. "Side effects include extremely painful migraines and severe drowsiness. You absolutely *must* stay awake until all of the potion has been taken, else your magic will never return. You will need help—you won't be able to do it on your own."

Nicole nodded. This didn't sound fun.

"After you take the potion, you'll be unconscious for several days. Make sure you start the process in a place where you'll be safe." He put a hand on her arm.

WITHHOLD

"Before you leave, I feel impressed to remind you again to trust your instincts. Nicole, there are people out there who need to be saved, who will be a great asset to your team, and you will be sorely tempted to ignore them in exchange for those dear to you. You *must* put aside your feelings and reach out to them, as you are the only one who can offer them help."

Nicole swallowed, her palms becoming clammy. What did Onyev know that he wasn't telling her?

He took a breath. "That's all—I wish you luck."

CHAPTER FIFTEEN

෩ ♦ ඤ

Nicole thanked him and left, wondering about his words of advice and where she could possibly go that would be guaranteed safe for several days. Earth was out of the question, and so was Eklaron. Well, most of it. Would the Fat Lady mind if Nicole hung out there? Or maybe she could join the Makalos in their village.

Nicole thought about her options as she returned to Jacob, figuring the Fat Lady was her best bet, as from what she'd heard, the Lorkon had never been able to break the woman's defenses. She'd holed herself up in that cabin for years and years and could probably do it again.

Jacob and Nicole returned to the Fat Lady's cabin, and Nicole told everyone there what Onyev had said. Austin was disappointed that it would take so long and would cause her pain. Coolidge, Azuriah, and the Fat

WITHHOLD

Lady agreed that the best place for Nicole would be the Fat Lady's cabin. It was decided that Jacob would stick around while Nicole took the potion in case anything bad happened, and in the meantime, Coolidge, Austin, and Azuriah would return to the bone dimension and continue recruiting help.

Austin wasn't happy with the plans. He wanted to stay with Nicole, but she and Coolidge had disagreed—they needed him more where everything was happening, and Nicole would be safe. If the potion killed her, she didn't want him to watch. And he probably wouldn't be able to do anything to help her through the pain. It would be horrible for him.

Once Nicole was set up on the Fat Lady's dusty couch, Austin gave her a kiss goodbye, the sadness and hesitation in his eyes betraying his confident exterior.

"I love you," he whispered, brushing her cheek with his finger. "Please, please take care of yourself."

Nicole nodded. "You too." She raised her hand with the ring on it. "Send positive thoughts, and I'll do the same. I have a feeling we'll both need them."

After the men left, not including Jacob, the Fat Lady began administering the potion. It took a full day to get all of the doses into Nicole.

The headaches began the minute that first teaspoon hit her stomach, and the pain was absolutely horrible. When Onyev said it would cause her migraines, he wasn't kidding. They split across her scalp, making her throw up multiple times. The Fat Lady had to cover all of her windows with heavy cloths because even the slightest light increased Nicole's pain a hundredfold. The entire time Nicole was taking the potion, neither Jacob nor the Fat Lady were able to speak to her. The slightest sound—especially voices—caused too much pain.

And the exhaustion—the exhaustion. It was uncontrollable. Nicole's body seemed to know that if it just relaxed, just let go, just succumbed to the need for sleep, the pain she was inflicting on it would be resolved. Her body fought to slip into dreamland, and she fought just as hard to stay awake.

Any time Jacob saw her eyes droop, he flicked her with a rubber band. It was the only thing that pulled her out of her pain-ridden stupor enough to wake up her mind.

Nicole spent most of the time on the Fat Lady's couch, breathing in through her nose and out through her mouth, a cold compress across her forehead. The Fat Lady spent most of *her* time inching her way back and forth from the kitchen sink to the couch, replacing the warm, used rags with cold ones. Jacob's job was to keep Nicole awake. He obviously hated sitting while the Fat Lady walked, but the Fat Lady simply wasn't fast enough to stop Nicole's eyes from shutting.

What a ridiculous, stupid ordeal Nicole was forced to go through because of one evil man. She couldn't wait to get her hands on him. The minute her powers returned, she'd destroy him.

With the help of the Great Ones, of course.

She couldn't entertain thoughts of revenge for long, though—the energy required was enough to induce an agony-filled stupor of exhaustion. As a result, she let her mind wander wherever it wanted to go—the path of least

WITHHOLD

resistance and all of that.

Finally, she'd taken the entire potion and was able to sleep.

The first thing she noticed when she drifted off was that she wasn't really sleeping. It was sort of a consciously unconscious state she entered—as if she was stuck in her brain, aware of everything her body was going through.

The second thing she recognized was pain, and so much more of it. What she'd felt earlier was nothing. Why hadn't Onyev warned her that sleeping wouldn't relieve it? The headaches spread, pulsing through her spine, down her limbs, and into her extremities, reaching and extending to her toes and fingers until her entire body was drenched in an all-encompassing migraine.

Weeks, months, years flew by—she was sure of it—while she begged and pleaded with whoever was listening to end her life, to relieve her of the pain, to take it away.

The pain increased until Nicole opened her eyes, trying to wake up. She didn't care about her magic anymore. It wasn't worth it—the agony, the responsibility of Shonlin, none of it. Onyev could take the sphere back. She'd *force* him to accept it.

Nicole was surprised that the Fat Lady's surroundings didn't greet her when she woke up. Instead, strange symbols floated in the air around her. They were almost like Chinese characters, but had a sort of Arabic flair to them. They glowed gold in the hazy murkiness that surrounded them. She watched them for several moments. She reached out, hesitating before touching the one nearest her. It had a warm sensation around it.

The moment she made contact with it, a gentle breeze tickled over her. It was pleasant, familiar, and welcoming. It brought comfort and happiness, making her eyes fill with tears. How she needed that comfort!

It didn't take long for the pain to return, though, and craving another respite, Nicole reached for the next symbol, also close. Once again, warmth rushed over her, but instead of a gentle breeze like the first symbol, feathery dust tumbled across her hand, face, and body. It wasn't unpleasant, even though dirt should have been, and it didn't seem to stick to her. She was able to shake it away easily. Again, the comfort was short-lived, and her pain came back.

The next symbol was just out of reach. Nicole tried to grasp it, and her headache increased. She hesitated, shocked, unsure what to do. She contemplated the symbol for several moments, her pain and headache increasing, making it difficult to think. This one wasn't glowing like the first two had. Should she leave it alone, or should she continue trying to get it?

Something about the symbol beckoned her, invited her to come. And realizing she might regret it, that she might be foolish for doing so, Nicole stretched for it once more. Pain flooded her system, making her gasp, but it was only intense for a brief moment before her fingers finally touched the symbol, drawing it toward herself. She felt power rush into her brain, heart, and soul while water sprinkled over her. It didn't leave her wet—it was almost as if it hadn't touched her, even though she'd felt it.

Nicole's mouth dropped open. She knew what the

WITHHOLD

symbols represented. They were the four elemental powers—they had to be. Staring at that last symbol and knowing that it represented Fire, Nicole wondered if she touched it and pulled it to herself, would she be granted the power it represented? Had the other symbols given her the other elemental magic? Was that why Water had been more difficult than Wind and Earth?

The pain was returning, but Nicole forced it to the back of her mind. She *would* get that last symbol!

Preparing herself mentally, she stretched as far as she could. It was much farther than the others. She reached again, straining. The pain pushed itself to the forefront of her mind, and her eyes began watering. Her head pounded. Her tendons and ligaments began to burn painfully. Then the migraine that encompassed her entire body returned, and she screamed at the intense pain.

Still, she persisted. The opportunity to grasp her powers was here, right now, and there was *no way* she'd miss it, regardless of how much it hurt.

The headache was blinding. She couldn't see the symbol anymore. Still, she stretched. Her muscles started cramping, her lungs felt like they were about to burst, and her heart constricted, making it feel like something was squeezing her chest. She began to pass out, lights flashing in her eyes.

CHAPTER SIXTEEN

☙ ◆ ❧

Blackness and pain collapsed over her at the same moment Nicole grasped the edge of the symbol, pulling it closer.

The power embraced her body and soul. Fire rushed over her, making every inch of her tingle. The pain was washed away immediately after, giving her an enormous rush of endorphins.

And suddenly, she was awake, her body and mind energized, her heart invigorated. She whooped in excitement.

"That was *amazing*!" she exclaimed, or at least tried to. Nicole frowned—even though she felt alert and attentive, her body was sluggish to respond. She hoped that would wear off soon.

"You're awake!" Lizzie said, dropping to her knees next to where Nicole lay on the couch.

WITHHOLD

The Fat Lady, Akeno, and Jacob hovered at the edge of the room.

"Keitus has fully enslaved earth—all dimensions of it," Jacob said.

Nicole couldn't think about Keitus right then. She had to know if what she'd seen—what she'd done—in her dream or vision had been real.

Her magic obeyed her the moment she knew what she wanted. A fire lit right in the middle of the air above her. Nicole felt a grin stretch across her face. She was a Silver now!

When Lizzie looked up and saw the fire, she gasped. "Holy cow, woman!" she said. "What *happened* while you were unconscious?"

Nicole thought about it. The amount of work, the pain she'd gone through to get those last elements must have equaled the pain and work she would've had to do in real life, but over a much shorter period of time. She'd definitely earned it. She whispered a thanks first to Onyev and then to Keitus. There was no way he would have been able to predict that by stealing her magic, he would make her a hundred times stronger. She knew her mastery of all the elements was perfect. The way they danced in the air around her, practically begging her to command them—none of that had happened before. This was so amazing.

"I—I think I'm a Silver now," she said.

"That's so *cool*," Lizzie said.

"Where are Austin, Coolidge, and the others?" Nicole asked.

Jacob rubbed the back of his neck, not meeting her

gaze. "I'm unable to see earth, except briefly here and there. It seems Keitus is using his powers to hide the entire planet from my vision. But what I *have* seen has been horrible. People are being enslaved, tortured, and killed."

Nicole didn't want to ask the question, but it tumbled out anyway. "What does this have to do with Austin and Coolidge?"

Lizzie regarded Nicole with serious eyes. "They insisted on going back to fight."

Nicole's heart stopped beating and she felt the blood in her veins stop. "No! They'll be destroyed! I need to see what's going on. Now!" Why had they gone back? What could they gain by fighting?

Jacob made a calming motion with his hands. "They're fine—I was able to pierce Keitus's blocks a couple of hours ago. But we have to get help. The last thing they said was to recruit as many Silvers as possible. We need to start doing that."

Nicole shook her head. "They shouldn't be fighting. We have to get them out of there."

"What we *need* to do," Lizzie said, "is find more people who can support us—help others before everyone friendly is enslaved. Not just so they can fight Keitus with us, but so we can approach the Great Ones without worrying we'll be fried." Lizzie looked at Nicole. "Because I *know* that's high on your agenda."

Nicole nodded. Lizzie was right. Their team wasn't strong enough—they needed more power and knowledge before they even tried talking to the Great Ones. And how would they go about doing that, anyway? No one had

WITHHOLD

ever given her instructions on finding their dimension.

"I've been searching for friendly magical people," Jacob said. "Those who would be powerful enough to help in some way, and I can't find any that haven't been enslaved already."

"What about that Silver on the other planet?" Lizzie asked. "He was close to Restarting. Maybe we could trigger his Restart, stay around to make sure he doesn't die when it happens, then have him help us."

"No," Nicole said, shaking her head, even as her heart warmed at the idea. Why did it warm? Was it what they were supposed to do? Her thoughts raced to follow Lizzie's. She knew she'd have to approach the Great Ones eventually—she *knew* it. And the Silver was a slave of the Agarchs, who were servants to the Great Ones. Would he know how to find their dimension?

Still, she continued her argument. "It's too much of a risk, especially if his Restart ends up being a bad one. We need people who can help us now."

"Have you considered that maybe *he* needs *us*?" Lizzie asked.

Onyev's words from earlier sprang into Nicole's mind, and she closed her eyes, picturing the old Makalo and the concern on his face as he advised her to help those who needed her. He'd said she was the only one who could offer that help.

But maybe it wouldn't be one-way. Maybe the Silver would be able to help them too. Even though she hated putting off finding and bringing Austin, Coolidge, and the others back, she knew Lizzie was right. They needed to rescue the Silver. She decided not to voice her feelings where the Great Ones were concerned.

"If we take him to Onyev," Nicole said, "do you think he could trigger a Restart?"

"I'm not sure." Jacob glanced at the Fat Lady. "Do you know?"

She shrugged, her actions back to normal speed. Nicole noticed that she wasn't holding the walking stick anymore. "Arete magic is very different from what we have here. Onyev might not be able to help."

"But he helped me get my powers back," Nicole said.

"It's definitely worth a try," Jacob said. "Let's at least get the Silver out before Keitus controls his world too. We might be able to heal him and get his help physically, if not magically."

The others agreed, and they started getting ready to leave. Only the Fat Lady would stay behind.

The sooner they rescued this guy, the sooner Nicole could find Austin.

CHAPTER SEVENTEEN

ೞ ✦ ಌ

Jacob opened a link from the Fat Lady's cabin to a very familiar door that Nicole had hoped she'd never see again. She stepped through to the other world, feeling butterflies swarming in her stomach. The nervousness only partially subsided while she, Lizzie, Akeno, and Jacob came up with a plan. They would approach the compound quietly, watching for Agarchs. Akeno would set up doors everywhere while Jacob Time-Saw as Nicole and Lizzie went to find the Silver. The moment Nicole and Lizzie had him, Jacob would open a link to the closest door, pull them through, then take them all back to the Fat Lady's cabin.

Jacob stayed behind, near the door they'd come through, and Akeno set off on his own to begin enlarging doors. Nicole and Lizzie followed soon after, moving through the underbrush. After making sure the way was clear, they headed down the path that led to the compound.

Nicole's eyes widened as she took in the scene before them—what awaited them. Groups of monsters were everywhere. It was easy to see that those groups were organized according to rank as they prepared for battle. She shouldn't have been surprised that Keitus would be commanding the monsters in this dimension.

She and Lizzie stepped off the path and dropped to their knees near a dirt pile where they could watch the compound without being spotted. The last time Nicole had come to this place, she'd gone *through* the dirt to reach the buildings. Would that work again? She pushed outward magically, sensing the little village. Her reach had grown so far—she could feel the entire compound and all of the magical creatures in it. Holy cow—that was huge. Last time, she'd struggled with sensing that there *were* magical beings in this place.

Closing her eyes, forcing herself to focus, she narrowed in on the dirt itself. The monsters must have anticipated another arrival because they'd hardened it a ton since the last time she'd been there. It wasn't soft and moist anymore, and without knowing her new magical limits, Nicole wasn't willing to waste time trying to push through it.

Aware that Lizzie was waiting for her, she briefly considered rushing the compound with a surprise elemental attack. But again, not knowing what her magic could do—how far she could push it—was a huge detriment. Too many of the monsters were powerful and possibly more advanced. It was too much of a gamble.

Nicole glanced at the clouds. They weren't the usual

WITHHOLD

rust red she'd come to expect on this planet. Instead, they were a blackened brown, and she wondered how much control Keitus already had here. Her powers let her know that the clouds held hardly any moisture at all—what did they consist of, if not water?

Nicole watched as Akeno continued setting up doors around the perimeter of the city, and she could sense Jacob's magic behind her as he Time-Saw. She and Lizzie needed to get going.

"What's the plan?" Lizzie whispered.

Nicole shook her head. "I'm not sure, honestly." She looked at her best friend. "Do you have any ideas?"

"Well, kind of," Lizzie said. "I mean, look at all those huts. There are creatures about our shape and size going in them in underclothes and coming out fully armored."

Nicole narrowed her eyes, thinking through Lizzie's implications. "Kind of like *Lord of the Rings*?"

Lizzie grinned. "Exactly."

"Which hut should we go into?" Nicole asked, grateful she wasn't alone in making plans.

"I think we should try that one."

Lizzie pointed subtly, and Nicole was surprised to see the hut she chose wasn't the closest.

"Why that one?"

"Because it's being used, but nowhere near as often as the ones closer to us. I know it has armor in it 'cause I've seen at least two demons enter and exit. But I've only seen the two, so I know it's not busy."

Nicole watched the hut for several moments. "I like it. Let's go."

She waited until the majority of the monsters were

looking in a different direction, then she created a dust storm with enough dirt in it to mask their figures as they dashed across the field toward the hut. At the same time, Nicole made other dirt devils on either side of them, wanting it to look like they'd happened spontaneously.

Nicole's heart pounded, more out of fear than exertion, but she and Lizzie reached the hut fine. They were out of breath and covered in dust and sweat when they ducked into the leather enclosure. She expected to find monsters inside, but no one was there. The two girls quickly rummaged through the available pieces, selecting ones that were roughly their size, then helped each other with ties and buckles.

The armor was heavy—very heavy—and it stank like body odor, blood, and sewage. Nicole's stomach curled, and she had to take shallow breaths to limit the amount of stench that entered her nose.

Before leaving the hut, Nicole pulled what water she could from the air and mixed it with dirt, then she and Lizzie spread the mud on their arms and faces, trying to disguise the fact that they were human.

Once they were fully covered in mud and armor, Nicole mentally searched for the Silver. She found his pulse almost immediately. He was close to the main hut, about halfway across the compound from where she and Lizzie were.

Nicole gave Lizzie's hand a quick squeeze, then they started toward that hut, blending in with the other creatures that milled around the compound. Nicole recognized the Silver soon as she saw him. She couldn't believe it was possible, but he was even more emaciated

WITHHOLD

now than he had been the last time she'd seen him. He was skin and bones. His lips were cracked and bleeding. His skin was flaking, and several patches of his hair had fallen out.

Onyev had told Nicole to trust her feelings and instincts, and looking at the Silver now, she knew they'd made the right choice in coming here to rescue him. There was something about him that told her he was important, that he would be integral to the future of Aretes on earth. She didn't know why she hadn't sensed that the first time she'd met him, nor why it was important for her to know now, but she appreciated it just the same.

Not waiting to see if the Silver would react to their appearance or call for help, Nicole commanded some of her magic to silence him, then she grabbed him by the arm, pulling him toward the door of the main hut. She hoped Jacob was watching and would be ready.

The Silver struggled until his eyes landed on Lizzie. Then he froze, his mouth hanging open, as he stared at her. Recognition flooded his features.

Nicole paused. Why was he looking at Lizzie like that? He'd never seen her before—Nicole was sure of it. Her best friend hadn't been to this world before. Not only that, but Lizzie was covered in armor and mud. How did this man recognize her?

Lizzie flushed under the attention, but didn't say anything as she grabbed the Silver's other arm and pulled him with Nicole.

They made their way to the door. After everything Nicole had been through on this world, she expected to have a great deal of difficulty in getting out again. But nobody seemed to notice them. Nicole wondered if she and Lizzie had even needed to disguise themselves at all.

The Silver was easy to subdue, and his strength fled his limbs quickly after Nicole and Lizzie began pulling him. Instead, the girls found themselves half carrying him as he lost energy. Nicole's heart clenched as she thought of what he'd gone through. The poor guy.

The door popped open just as they reached it, and Jacob ushered them through. He raised his eyebrow, staring at Nicole and Lizzie.

"We had to blend in somehow," Lizzie said.

Jacob looked back at the compound before he shut the door. "Something tells me you didn't need it."

"That thought crossed my mind as well," Nicole said. "We could have gone in there wearing Cinderella dresses and I don't think it would have mattered. They didn't pay us any attention."

Jacob keyed them to the Fat Lady's cabin, and Nicole and Lizzie led the Silver down the hall into her living room, where they helped him to the couch. He took one look at his new surroundings and slid to the floor, his head in his hands.

Nicole and Lizzie looked at each other. What now? Why had they felt so strongly that he needed to be rescued?

Jacob didn't seem too concerned with the Silver. Nicole wondered if he was giving the man space. Nicole touched the Silver's shoulder and said, "Are you okay?"

The man shook his head, and Nicole gasped. Had he understood her? She hadn't thought he actually spoke English.

WITHHOLD

He collapsed to the floor, unconscious. Nicole dropped next to him, feeling for a pulse. It was faint. She looked around for Akeno, but he wasn't there.

Nicole jumped to her feet. "Where's Akeno? Did we leave him back on the other planet?"

"No," Jacob said. "His parents got a Minya through to us—they needed his help, so I keyed him to Taga Village. He has to take care of his own people."

Nicole knitted her eyebrows, staring at the Silver. "We've got to heal him. Do you have any sap?"

Jacob shook his head. "Not enough—we'd have to cover his entire body. What he needs is to be shrunk and put in a Minya container."

"That's what I was hoping would happen, but without Akeno . . . What do we do?"

"The best we can. I'll give him a quick examination and take care of any injuries he has, but—"

"Don't worry about him," the Fat Lady said from her kitchen. "He needs rest, food, and water. I'll care for him while you worry about getting everyone out of Keitus's grasp." She motioned for them to join her. "But first, food."

Nicole's stomach grumbled in response to that, letting her know she was hungry. Weird. She hadn't had an appetite since this whole ordeal had started. How was she going to eat now?

"I need to check on my family first," Jacob said. His eyes glazed over as he apparently Time-Saw somewhere. He returned, focusing his gaze on Nicole, his jaw working, his eyes filling with tears. "My parents . . . Austin, Mr. Coolidge. They've been enslaved. All of them."

Nicole jumped to her feet. "What? Where? We have to get them!" She shouldn't have let them stay on earth so long! What would she do if something happened to Austin?

Jacob nodded. "This is going to be difficult."

"Why?" Nicole asked. "Where are they?"

"It looks like Keitus's minions dug a hole under the street in front of Professor Coolidge's house. That's where they'd all been fighting. The only way into the stupid cell is through the roof, and the whole place is teeming with monsters." He shook his head. "Our people are all covered in blood. Some of them didn't move while I was watching—I can't tell if they're alive." He looked at Nicole, his eyes red. "Including Austin, my mom, and Mr. Coolidge."

Nicole felt like someone had punched her in the chest. Her heart practically stopped beating, and pain radiated everywhere, similar to what she'd experienced while sleeping off the toxins. She blinked several times, forcing her tears away. She struggled not to scream, trying to maintain a calm exterior. "I—I thought they were supposed to be in the bone dimension. Why did *everyone* go to earth?"

"I'm not sure of their reasoning," Jacob said. "I wasn't there for the conversation. Dad just told me they weren't willing to sit and wait while everything and everyone they loved was destroyed."

"Why aren't they being frozen or killed like everyone else?" Lizzie asked.

Jacob only shook his head—he obviously didn't know.

WITHHOLD

"Probably because Keitus knows we'll try to rescue them," Nicole said. "He's going to use them as bait or leverage for something." She got up and started pacing through the Fat Lady's huge stacks of papers and books. "This is ridiculous. We can't leave them there, and we can't attack Keitus."

Jacob stared at her for a moment. "What do you think we should do?"

"Storm the place," Nicole said. "Do something he doesn't think a bunch of students are capable of doing. We'll destroy his little guard and get our people back. And then . . . and then we'll disappear from his view."

"How do we do that?" Lizzie asked.

Nicole motioned for Jacob to lead the way to the door. "I'm not sure, but we'll figure something out."

"Where am I taking us?" Jacob asked when he'd reached the door and pulled out his key.

Nicole's limbs began shaking with anger. The energy she'd stored up was begging to be released, to destroy something. And it was about to be put to good use.

She grabbed the umbrella and handed it to Lizzie to use, talking to Jacob. "Key us to Coolidge's house and keep the link open. I'll blast my way to that cell. I don't care if it overwhelms me—we're getting everyone out."

CHAPTER EIGHTEEN
※ ✦ ※

Jacob opened the link, and without waiting to see what was on the other side, without knowing what she was getting herself into, Nicole stormed through, gathering as much magic as she could, then roared as she charged toward the group of monsters standing in Coolidge's yard.

Arms spread wide, Nicole magically pulled all the debris from the surrounding area and blasted it at the monsters. The resulting explosion was so massive, the monsters were flung over half a mile away. Nothing remained between Nicole and the entrance to that cell.

She turned to face it. It was a simple wooden plank with large metal hinges. She wasn't sure how it was affixed to the street, and she didn't care.

Pushing outward with her powers, Nicole grabbed everything that formed the top of the cell, including the dirt and wood, and thrust it away, exposing the injured prisoners. She raced to the edge of the hole and jumped down inside. Jacob hadn't been kidding—it was *very* small. Professor Coolidge, Hayla, Austin, and several others were there, including Austin's parents. Many of them were piled on top of each other, barely aware that anything had happened around them.

Nicole couldn't reach Austin without stepping over Hayla, and she knew the pregnant woman needed to be cared for first. She gingerly touched her shoulder. "Hayla? Are you okay?"

Hayla stirred, mumbling, her eyes opening. Nicole's shoulders slumped in relief. Hayla was still alive. Azuriah stepped forward—his robes were torn, but otherwise, he didn't seem to be injured. Together, he, Lizzie, and Nicole helped Hayla to her feet and walked her back through the link to the Fat Lady's cabin.

They immediately returned as Jacob called for help with Coolidge. Blood streamed from a wound on the professor's forehead, and mud caked the side of his face. He didn't respond to anything Nicole or Jacob did, but he had a faint pulse.

Nicole looked at the other injured people—there were at least ten of them. "We can't do this fast enough," she said. "We need a Makalo to shrink everyone—we'll never move them in time."

Jacob nodded. "I was thinking the same thing. Let me go see if one can help."

He jogged away, and Nicole turned back to her professor. They needed to do something about that head injury! He'd lost so much blood.

Jacob returned, Akeno following closely.

"I can't stay for long. I'm going to shrink everyone so you can carry them out and find a place for them to rest and heal."

Akeno looked like he'd been crying, and Nicole's heart ached for him and what he and his family must have been going through.

The Makalo waved off her concern, though, and immediately got to work. He shrank Coolidge and walked away, carrying the professor while Nicole and Azuriah stepped to the next person and Jacob and Lizzie helped an injured man to his feet.

Tears welled up in Nicole's eyes when she saw her fiancé. His face was so swollen, she barely recognized him. His hair was matted with dried blood, and his shoulder appeared to be dislocated. One of his legs was also awkwardly bent.

Sobs welled up inside Nicole, and she had to breathe hard to force them away. What had those monsters done to her people? Her anger returned, making her arm shake as she brushed Austin's forehead. The wounded body next to him disappeared as Akeno shrank another person.

Austin woke up, staring at Nicole with confusion. He struggled for a moment, trying to get to his feet, but she shook her head, gently holding him down.

"No, Austin, no," she said. "Stay still. You're fine—we're all going to be okay." Her lower lip trembled as she said this, and she wondered if she was speaking the truth. *Were* they going to be okay?

Akeno shrank Austin last and handed him to Nicole. She held him carefully in her palm, making sure he

WITHHOLD

wouldn't get jostled. He slipped out of consciousness as she walked back to the Fat Lady's cabin.

Once everyone was through the link, Jacob closed the door behind them, and Nicole surveyed the cabin. With Hayla, Azuriah, the Fat Lady, Lizzie, Nicole, the Silver, and Jacob at their full sizes, there was barely any room to move. How were they going to care for so many injured people in a place that didn't have enough food or beds for everyone?

Lizzie voiced Nicole's concerns. "There's got to be somewhere we can take these people."

Nicole rubbed her eyes with her free hand, nodding. She didn't have an answer.

The Fat Lady tapped her shoulder, and Nicole turned to her. "The magic on my cabin is faltering—Keitus must know this is where we've been hiding. The shields weren't designed to protect more than one or two people under direct attack. We need to leave."

"Does anyone know of a place Keitus doesn't have access to?" Akeno asked.

The Fat Lady looked like she was about to respond for a moment, but then she didn't. She shook her head. "Nothing that he wouldn't eventually find."

An idea popped into Nicole's mind, and she hesitated as she pondered what she was about to say. Would he be okay with having all these people there? "I know where we can go, but he's not going to like it very much." She exhaled slowly. "But I first have to get the necklace back."

She didn't have to think very long before the sphere appeared in her open hand. Taking care not to injure him further, she gently placed Austin into Lizzie's free hand, then let the sphere hover in front of her and thought about Shonlin, the visions immediately jumping into her mind. The guardian was ready for her.

"What do you seek?"

"I need the necklace I brought here several days ago."

The guardian led her to the shelf where she'd sealed Sanso's necklace.

The Ember God had asked her to join him and desert her friends, putting this whole Keitus ordeal behind her. She'd said no, but he'd given her the necklace, saying it would help her find him if she ever changed her mind.

She took the necklace back to the Fat Lady's cabin. "Now I just need figure out how to use it," she said.

Nicole turned the necklace around and around in her hand, peering at it, trying to get it to show her Sanso's world. She thought hard about him, hoping that would do something. But it didn't. Did it require magic? And if so, what kind? Sanso controlled fire—maybe that was the way to get it to work.

She sent a small flame to the necklace, exhilaration that she could even do that flowing over her as she tried to ignite it. That didn't work either.

As a last resort, Nicole traced her finger along the edge of the metal, thinking about Sanso and her goal to reach him. She gasped when the necklace warmed in her hand. Instead of a glowing path appearing in her mind, as was the case with Shonlin, she felt a sudden desire to get up and walk toward the door. She did so.

The moment she got there, her hand reached for the knob, about to open it, but then she hesitated, and another

WITHHOLD

urge hit her. She wanted to take the key from Jacob. She turned around.

"Jacob?" she called.

"Yeah?"

"I think I need the key. Or at least I need you to open a link somewhere."

Jacob joined her, pulling it out of his pocket as he did. "Where do you want to go?"

Nicole shrugged. She had no idea. The urge to leave intensified as Jacob and his key drew near. "Um, I don't know. Would the key work if you told it to take me where the necklace is leading us?"

Jacob quirked an eyebrow, but turned to the door anyway. "Take me where Nicole needs to go." He twisted the key in the lock and opened the door. Nicole felt relief rush over her as she saw what was on the other side. Instead of the field, path, and lake that were just outside the Fat Lady's cabin, a dark stone interior greeted them. The walls were damp with glistening water.

Following the intense desire that overwhelmed her again, Nicole crossed the threshold into the other world, trusting that her friends would follow. They did.

The room was small and tight—more of a hallway than a room. A door was at the other end, and Nicole opened it, still following those needs and desires. The handle was dry, even though it also glistened. She glanced at the walls, wondering if they were covered in something that made them look wet or if they actually dripped water. She almost touched the stone, but thought better of it. She didn't know what the substance was, and if it wasn't water, she didn't want to risk hurting herself.

This door opened to a long, deserted hallway with pillars lining it. The pillars weren't there for decoration—Nicole could tell they were supporting the roughly cut ceiling. Just beyond the pillars on either side was a crevice so deep that she couldn't see the bottom of it. She didn't step closer to peer down. Light filtered from above, where fires burned in trenches that lined the top of the room.

Nicole glanced back, checking on her friends as they came through the link and Jacob shut the door. Each of them carried an injured body in both hands. *Please be able help us, Sanso,* she thought.

CHAPTER NINETEEN

৪০ ♦ ෬

Yet another door needed to be opened at the end of this hall. Nicole cringed when a pungent smell—acrid smoke of some kind—filled her nostrils and burned her nose, making her cough.

The room was full of ancient artifacts. Dusty tomes graced shelves, and old leather chairs were scattered throughout. It was dark and dingy, but appeared to be large enough to hold everyone in Nicole's group, including those who were injured. Sanso was seated in a chair opposite from the door, staring at Nicole in surprise.

"I didn't expect you to come," he said. He jumped to his feet and crossed to her, taking her into his arms. With his face buried in her neck, he mumbled something else, but Nicole stepped away.

She glanced behind her. "I didn't come alone. We need help—we need a place to stay. Until things are resolved with Keitus."

Sanso chuckled. "So, you're finally willing to believe what I said about him *always* getting what he wants?"

Nicole didn't respond. She didn't know how to, and she'd already sacrificed enough pride recently. Instead, she ushered her friends into the room. She turned to Sanso. "We barely got out on time."

"And let me guess," Sanso said. "You're still determined to go back and defeat him." It was more of a statement than a question.

She shrugged. They both knew the answer.

Nicole motioned to her friends. "We've got a lot of injured people—some are barely alive."

Without her even having to ask him, Sanso started gathering cots and beds, pulling them from where they'd been stacked inside a storage area, shoving chairs aside to make room. He acted as if it was normal to have such a large group of people in his place. And maybe it was—Nicole didn't know.

Akeno enlarged everyone, apologizing for not having any Minya containers, and Nicole helped get the injured people situated. She spent extra time with Austin, cleansing the blood from his face and making sure his injuries weren't getting infected. He needed clean clothes, antibiotics, and bandages. She wasn't sure where he'd get any of those. Sanso was still wearing the same outfit he'd had on when she met him, so he obviously didn't have extra clothes lying around.

While Sanso was helping set everybody up and making sure they were all comfortable, he told Nicole a little about the world where they were now were.

WITHHOLD

Apparently, it was uninhabitable by most magical creatures—Aretes and Ember Gods were the most powerful beings that could comfortably live there, which was why Keitus wouldn't ever come. Not only that, but the world also prevented people who weren't at least part human from dwelling there. When Nicole asked about the Makalos, Sanso explained that they had enough human in their genes to cross the threshold.

She hadn't realized that the Makalos even *had* human in them. She wondered if they knew.

Once the injured were resting on cots, Sanso showed Nicole around the place. There were several random rooms not being used for anything, a cramped old kitchen—with a sink, a wood-burning stove, and a drain in the floor—and restroom facilities that stank really badly. Sanso gave her an apologetic expression, but didn't say anything. The door they'd come through led outside. He didn't take her there, though.

"We don't go out very often," he said.

Nicole didn't ask why, though she was dying to know. The way Sanso said it made it seem very final—like something she wouldn't be able to argue. Maybe he'd tell her eventually.

"Where are the other Ember Gods?" she asked.

"They're scattered throughout the world." Sanso rubbed the back of his neck. "We don't interact with each other very often."

Nicole remembered that those who had been closest to Sanso had been murdered by Keitus when he'd decided he didn't need their help anymore.

"Do you have any medicines or medical items?"

They needed to take care of her friends.

"No," Sanso said. "I mean, I've got chicken soup and other stuff that would probably help, but nothing that would heal them. Ember Gods don't get injured very often, and when we do, we don't respond to the same sort of things other species do."

Nicole was disappointed. They'd have to do their best. Maybe Jacob could raid a hospital or bring Kaede sap back from Taga Village.

"Are you hungry?" he asked.

The Fat Lady had been about to feed them. Yes, Nicole was hungry. But was it fair for her to impose on him when there were so many of them?

Sanso laughed when he saw her hesitation. "Come on, Nicole. I invited you to stay here. What sort of host would I be if I didn't also offer your guests the same accommodations?"

"Do you have enough, though?"

"Perhaps."

He beckoned for her to follow him back to the kitchen area. Instead of preparing food himself, he rang a bell.

A little door opened in the wall nearest Nicole, and a small creature entered. It was about three feet tall, humanoid, and female. She had ears on her cheeks, a long nose, and small eyes.

"Please fix Nicole and her guests something to eat," Sanso said, motioning to Nicole.

The woman curtsied, looking up at Nicole. "What would you like?"

Nicole hesitated. "What are the options?"

"Anything you want."

WITHHOLD

Sanso touched Nicole's arm. "Barbara is able to create food based on pictures. If you've got a picture of something edible, she'll be able to create it, even without the ingredients. It's sort of her magical ability."

Nicole pulled her phone from her back pocket and scrolled through the images on it. The only one of food she had was a shot she'd asked a waitress to take of her and Austin during their last date. It wasn't much, but it showed a half-eaten chicken, some soup, broccoli, and asparagus. She showed the phone to the woman.

"Very well," Barbara said.

Nicole stepped away, watching as the small woman began yanking pots and pans out of cupboards, pulling food from boxes, and a handful of what looked and smelled like—Nicole couldn't believe it—manure from a knapsack in the corner of the room. Rather than do everything separately, the woman threw it all into one of the bigger pots, then sprinkled some more of the manure on top. She muttered a few words, and with a poof, the stuff in the pot began bubbling and boiling.

The creature turned to Nicole and said, "Please excuse me while I continue."

Nicole nodded, understanding that she was being dismissed. She and Sanso left, shutting the door behind them. They returned to Nicole's group, silent the entire way. Nicole told her friends they would have food shortly.

She didn't tell them about the manure.

Twenty minutes later, the woman entered the room, carrying a stack of plates which Sanso took from her while Nicole, Lizzie, and Jacob set up a table. Sanso put the plates on it, along with cups, bowls, and silverware that the woman brought next.

Rather than serve the food as Nicole had expected, the woman sprinkled a little bit of the dirt on each plate and bowl. Once finished, she clapped her hands twice, and food appeared, steaming and ready to eat. Nicole's shoulders slumped in relief. It was perfect. It didn't smell a thing like manure, looked exactly like what she and Austin had eaten—still whole, though—and she was too hungry to turn her nose up at soup, chicken, broccoli, and asparagus.

It didn't take much encouragement for everyone to start eating. They were famished.

Nicole couldn't help but watch her friends. Hayla carefully spooned the soup into her mouth while Lizzie, Jacob, and Azuriah ate like they hadn't seen food in years. The Fat Lady had opted to stay in her cabin, reassuring Nicole that once everyone was gone, she'd be fine and that she'd send a Minya if anything happened.

Austin and Coolidge were still unconscious, as was the Silver. Nicole ached to help them, but it had been more than twenty-four hours since she'd last eaten, and she knew she needed strength. Once she'd taken care of herself, she'd turn her attention to them.

She'd nearly finished her meal when someone yelled on the other side of the room. A pillow was chucked through the air, narrowly missing hitting the table, followed closely by a book.

Nicole turned, seeing Sanso with his hands up, backing away from the Silver who had lunged to his feet, his chest rising quickly with his panicked breaths.

CHAPTER TWENTY

ঃ ✦ ☙

"Hey," Nicole said, jumping up. "It's okay. You're with friends—we're not going to hurt you."

The Silver stared at Nicole, his mouth working wordlessly. Then his eyes drifted across the room and landed on Lizzie. Nicole glanced at her best friend, realizing they hadn't yet had time to clean up. Lizzie had dirt smudges on her face, and her hair was matted. It didn't seem to matter—the man was looking at her like he was seeing an angel for the first time.

Lizzie met eyes with Nicole, a faint blush entering her cheeks. Her expression seemed to ask Nicole why the man was staring at her.

Nicole didn't know. She returned her attention to the Silver and took another step toward him. "Hi," she said. "I'm Nicole."

The Silver's eyes went back to her. He paused, then said in a deep voice, "Hi."

"You *do* speak English," Nicole said.

The man didn't respond, but just stared at her.

Nicole resisted the urge to fiddle with her hands, unsure what to do. Was he trying to make her uncomfortable, or did he just not know how to respond?

"Are you hungry?" she asked.

The Silver's eyes drifted to the table. Without waiting for an invitation, he stumbled across the room, took a seat, and started eating from an unclaimed plate.

Not knowing what else she could do, Nicole returned to her own seat and finished her meal.

Akeno sent Nicole an apologetic expression. "I'm sorry again that I couldn't bring anything else. All of the Minya containers are being used, and we ran out of Kaede sap."

Nicole shook her head. "Please, don't worry about it. You guys have a lot going on too." Her eyes widened. "Do you need to go back? Are the Makalos okay?"

He nodded. "Yes, in answer to both questions. We're no longer in immediate danger—we'd forgotten about the hole in our wall where the Sindons come and go. It's sealed up now, but we had a bad fight with some of Keitus's men who sneaked through first. I'll need to keep helping out. Making sure we really are safe."

Akeno fell silent, and the rest of the meal was uncomfortable. It didn't help that Sanso was there—he always seemed to make things weird—but with the Silver's presence, it was even more awkward.

Finally, everyone finished. Nicole and Lizzie helped Sanso return the dishes to the kitchen, where the woman began cleaning immediately. She refused help, so Sanso

WITHHOLD

and the girls went back to talk with those who were awake and well.

Nicole grinned when they entered the room. Jacob had opened a package of Kaede sap, and he and Akeno were applying it to those who'd been injured.

He looked up when the girls came in. "The Fat Lady found some sap in her cabin. It's not enough to heal anyone completely, so we decided to spread it around—see if we can make them all more comfortable."

Nicole felt tears prick her eyes. "This is so wonderful. Thank you so much."

He nodded. "I just wish the stuff in the castle hadn't been destroyed—Mom and Dad kept *so* much of it on hand."

Nicole wiped her face. "I know."

Keitus evidently knew about Kaede sap, and one of the first things he'd had his minions do was destroy it everywhere they went.

She took a breath and approached Austin's cot. He was still unconscious. She peeked under the bandages—the wounds were already healing. This time, she didn't try to stop the tears. She couldn't believe how close her fiancé had come to dying.

Nicole picked up Austin's hand—the one that wasn't injured—and held it in her lap, rubbing his fingers, letting him know she was there. She felt someone's eyes on her, and expecting it to be Sanso, looked up. It was the Silver. He was resting on a cot.

"So, what's your name?" Nicole asked him.

He glared at her. "I remember you."

"I'm not the enemy," Nicole said. Why was he acting

like this? She and her friends were on the good side. Those stupid Agarchs were the enemy.

The Silver let his gaze flit across the room to Lizzie, who was sitting in the corner near Hayla and Coolidge, pretending to read a book. Nicole didn't blame her—this guy was seriously awkward.

"Abel. My name is Abel."

Lizzie lifted her eyes from the book, meeting his gaze. "Like in the Bible?"

"Like in the Bible."

"I've never met anyone named that before," Lizzie said. "Is there a story behind your name?"

He frowned, turning away from her. "Yes. And that story is none of your business."

Nicole and Lizzie looked at each other. Lizzie rolled her eyes.

"So, tell us about yourself," Nicole said.

Abel glared at her before looking at Lizzie again. "Only if *she* wants me to."

Lizzie raised her eyebrows. "Why me?"

"I'm not at liberty to say." Abel suddenly found his hands very interesting.

Nicole frowned. "Why not? And why are you acting like you recognize her? It's not like you've ever met her before. She's never even been to that world—only I have."

Abel didn't look at her. "It doesn't matter. I still know her."

"How?" Lizzie asked. "*How* do you know me?"

"I'm not at liberty to say," he repeated, his eyes on his hands again.

WITHHOLD

Nicole sighed to herself, sitting back down. "Well, what *can* you tell us?"

Abel scowled. "I'm from earth—all Aretes are, originally. The monsters who had me in their possession kidnapped me once they realized who I was and what I was supposed to do." He mumbled something to himself, then said, "I performed certain tasks for them. And for other beings—things I . . ." He clamped his lips shut. "I've spent the last five years of my life acting as a slave to them."

"Where on earth are you from?" Lizzie asked.

Nicole smiled to herself at Lizzie's joke. Her friend didn't catch the pun in her question, and neither did Abel, who ran a hand through his hair.

"I'm not sure, honestly. My parents moved around a great deal. I think my dad might've been in the American military."

"Is anyone you know still alive?" Nicole asked. "Anyone you would like to go visit, let them know that you're safe?"

Abel shook his head abruptly. "No. There isn't. They were all destroyed five years ago." He glowered, looking even angrier now than he had before.

Nicole and Lizzie looked at each other, and an unspoken agreement ran between them—they weren't going to pursue conversation with this guy. He was a bit unhinged.

Once Azuriah finished checking a cut on his arm, he, Nicole, Lizzie, and Jacob pulled their chairs together to discuss their situation and make plans. Nicole had been disappointed to discover that Abel hadn't Restarted yet, but that didn't change the fact that he needed to be rescued. He'd refused Jacob's offer to take him to visit Onyev, and no one was willing to force time travel on him.

Nicole took a breath. "I don't even know where to begin. We need to stop Keitus. But how?"

"It's not like we can rely on anyone else," Jacob said. "We can't expect some random, powerful creature to come along and save us, not when Keitus has already taken over so many worlds."

"You're going to have to go to the Great Ones," Sanso said.

Nicole looked at the Ember God. He was sitting on the opposite side of the room from their group. She vaguely noticed that Abel was also paying attention.

"That's what I've been saying," she said. "But everybody keeps telling me we can't do it."

"Yeah, well, now we know it must happen," Azuriah said. "You're not doing it alone, though."

"No, she isn't," Lizzie said. "All of us—all who are healthy—are going."

"No way," Nicole said. "There is *no way* I'm letting you guys come. I've already gone up against them, I know what to expect, and I'm not letting you risk becoming their slaves."

Lizzie's face turned red. "When are you going to get it through that thick skull of yours that you're not *supposed* to do everything? You act like you're a hero all the time, trying to protect me and everyone else from doing dangerous things, and I'm tired of it! I'm tired of being treated like I'm some prissy, delicate, inexperienced . .

WITHHOLD

." She turned even redder as she fumbled for words. "... silly girl!"

Nicole's mind went blank. She opened her mouth to respond, but nothing came to her. Had she really been treating Lizzie that way? No, no. It wasn't possible. Lizzie could obviously hold her own—she'd stood against Helen just fine. And every time Nicole had seen a need to have Lizzie there or had seen that Lizzie's powers would help, she'd made sure Lizzie had been there.

"That's not what I've been doing," Nicole said. "You've come on many of these trips with us. I mean, you went to Salmon, you came with me to Romania, and you endured that horrible ladder to Renforth's world. I haven't ever deserted you!"

Lizzie started responding, but Jacob raised his hands, calming both of them. "Okay, okay," he said. "You're both right. Lizzie has been left out several times—"

"Not just because of me!" Nicole said.

"But she's also gone on a lot of these expedition things. Probably more than I have." He took a breath, obviously unwilling to let either girl take over the conversation again. "Nicole, you don't have a choice—Lizzie, Azuriah, and I are coming with you." He looked at Sanso and Abel. "The two of you are welcome to come as well." His eyes landed on Akeno. "And I need to take you back to your family."

Akeno nodded. "I'm really sorry—if I could help more, I would."

"It's okay. We appreciate what you've done." Jacob rubbed the back of his neck. "Either way, it doesn't matter who actually wants to go to the Great Ones' dimension.

We don't know how to get there."

"Yes, we do," Sanso said. "I'll show you the way when you're ready to leave. They created a path to their world on every planet. I've never been there—I can only tell you where that path is."

"What about the door to the kingdom?" Abel asked. "If the door doesn't know or recognize you, it won't grant you access."

Nicole's heart warmed—she'd been right. He would be the key. "You know how to get there?"

"Of course. I was enslaved by their servants for many years. I've held the door open multiple times, even for up to a full day."

Nicole felt hope rise in her chest. If Abel had done this before, they'd be okay. They'd be able to reach the Great Ones and beg them for help.

Realizing she wouldn't win this battle, she agreed to let the others go. They decided to head out first thing in the morning.

CHAPTER TWENTY-ONE

☙ ✦ ☙

Sanso showed everyone where they'd be sleeping, and as Nicole got ready for bed in a tiny room that she would be sharing with Lizzie, she couldn't stop feeling panicked about having Lizzie and Jacob go. Was it because she felt they were weaker? No! That couldn't be it. Jacob had proven himself multiple times, and definitely so had Lizzie. What, then? And was it her instincts warning her, or her protective nature?

Nicole lay across her bed, her feet hanging over the end of it, and stared at the dark stone ceiling above her. Like the walls in the other rooms here, this stone glistened like it was wet. She knew by now, though, that it wasn't water, but an undrinkable substance not found on earth. It wasn't poisonous, just annoying and pretty much everywhere. Seeing it on the stone was still a little weird.

Her thoughts drifted back to the argument she was

having with herself. If she was being honest, she knew she really *did* want to save Lizzie and Jacob from having to interact with the Great Ones.

Wait. *Interact with the Great Ones.* Nicole set up suddenly. Her instincts were right. Lizzie and Jacob *couldn't* go. Nicole was a guardian of Shonlin because she had *interacted with the Great Ones* and had been left unscathed. She knew from experience that most people who came into contact with the Great Ones were murdered or forced to serve them forever. Promises of riches and power polluted their minds until they no longer had control of themselves.

Nicole also knew that Azuriah would become a guardian of Shonlin. The fact that he hadn't been present at Lasia's trial said that in the present time, he hadn't yet met any of the Great Ones.

He was definitely supposed to go with Nicole. But what about Lizzie or Jacob? Would they be okay accompanying Nicole, but allow her to face the Great Ones alone? She knew they wouldn't—they'd find a way to follow her or force her to let them stay with her just in case.

Nicole looked across the room at Lizzie, who had fallen asleep almost as soon as her head hit the pillow. She slept peacefully, the worry lines erased from her face. Would she ever get over being left behind? Nicole bit the inside of her cheek, hesitating. This decision, especially after how Lizzie yelled at her earlier, might ruin their relationship. Lizzie might never trust her again.

It was worth it. Her friend's *life* was worth it. Nicole couldn't let anyone but herself, Azuriah, and Abel go. It

WITHHOLD

was too dangerous.

After making sure that Lizzie was in a deep sleep, Nicole sneaked out of the room, softly closing the door behind her. The hallway was dimly lit. She stepped down it quietly, then opened the door on the other end, knowing it would lead to the little kitchen. Sanso was sitting at a small table in the corner, nursing what looked to be some sort of an alcoholic beverage. He glanced up at her. "I figured I'd see you pretty soon."

"I can't let them come."

"I know. It's not in your nature to put those you love in danger."

"The Great Ones would never let them leave."

Sanso shrugged, getting to his feet and setting the cup on the table. "Come with me," he said, motioning for her to follow.

They went back to the main room, where all the tables and chairs had been put away and more cots pulled out so those who weren't injured would have a place to sleep. The room was crowded now. Nicole took a deep breath, looking over the people in her stewardship. *Please let the Great Ones listen.*

Azuriah and Jacob were both sound asleep. Sanso pointed at the Shiengol, indicating that Nicole should wake him. She headed that way while the Ember God went to Abel's side.

Nicole gently prodded Azuriah's shoulder. His eyes fluttered open, and for a moment, panic crossed his face before he recognized her. He swung his legs over the side of the bed, then stood up. After he and Abel were steady on their feet, the four of them left the room.

Once they'd returned to the kitchen, Nicole turned to the Shiengol and Abel and explained her reasoning behind leaving Lizzie and Jacob behind. She fudged the truth a bit—saying Azuriah was much more powerful than the others, leaving out the detail about already knowing he was a future guardian of Shonlin. He'd probably figure it out on his own, if he thought about it hard enough. He looked too tired to think logically, though.

Azuriah and Abel were both willing to leave right away, and Sanso quickly explained to the three of them how to find the link to the other world. He gave them food and water—enough for a couple days' journey. Nicole hoped they wouldn't be gone longer than that.

"Do any of you know how to ride horses?" Sanso asked.

All three of them nodded.

"Good. You can borrow mine. I have two."

He took them back the way they'd come when Jacob had first keyed them there, then opened the door to the outside world. Nicole saw immediately why the Ember Gods didn't go outside often. Three moons brightened the sky, casting blue light on the scene that greeted them, and that scene wasn't pleasant. More of that water-like stuff coated everything, and instead of dirt and paths, the ground was covered with jutting stones. Gnarled trees barely clung to life as their roots snaked through the rocks, struggling to find nourishment.

Sanso noticed Nicole looking at his front yard and explained, "I've tried several times to tame it, but the rocks here grow just as quickly as weeds do on your planet."

WITHHOLD

Rocks that grew? Fascinating. Nicole wished she could learn more about them, but instead of asking questions, she motioned for him to lead the way.

Sanso led them to a small barn behind the little house they'd just exited. The barn was carved into the side of the rocky hill.

"How do you keep the rocks from destroying it?" Nicole asked.

"Part of selling a dwelling on this planet includes a law to make it inhabitable. It's a magic that has been lost for hundreds of years, but the man who built this house set up the protections against the stone. I don't know what he did, but it has worked."

Sanso ducked into the small barn and emerged a few moments later, leading horses that also had to duck to exit. Nicole looked more closely at the barn, wondering how the horses survived in it. The thing was squat, windowless, and very dark. If these creatures didn't suffer from depression already, nothing would get them down.

"Just the two," Sanso said. "I wish I had more."

Nicole, Azuriah, and Abel looked at each other. Nicole groaned inwardly. She didn't want to ride with a strange guy who went back and forth between glaring at her and offering to help, which meant riding with Azuriah. But man, that was not something she would have chosen to do under different circumstances.

Sanso handed over the reins, and Nicole gave the first horse to Abel, then glanced at Azuriah. He seemed to know what was on her mind and was just as uncomfortable as she. But he didn't contradict her.

When Sanso brought the saddle and blanket out, Nicole got the horse ready, glad to see equipment she was familiar with. Without waiting for approval, she hoisted herself up into the saddle, then glanced at Azuriah. "Would you rather ride in front of me or behind?"

Azuriah glared at her. "Behind."

He took hold of the saddle and pulled himself up easily. She was relieved that he didn't put his arms around her. This whole situation was uncomfortable enough without that.

Sanso reviewed the instructions on how to reach their destination. Basically, they had to follow the trail in front of his house—the one Nicole still couldn't see, but which Sanso assured her the horses knew—for several hours, taking the left fork at every opportunity. Eventually, they would end up in the Great Ones' dimension.

"It's so close to where you live," Nicole said.

Sanso nodded. "This world isn't very big. And humans here come and go frequently, so there's more than one link."

"How will we know when we've reached their dimension?" Nicole asked.

Sanso pointed at Abel. "That's why you're bringing him, isn't it? I've never been there."

"Thank you so much for your help," she said.

Sanso frowned. "I'd still prefer it if you had come alone."

Nicole chuckled, then realized with a start that he hadn't flirted with her once since she'd arrived. He'd hugged her, but it hadn't really been flirtatious. He really *had* figured out that she wasn't interested in him, then.

WITHHOLD

After goodbyes and good lucks had been exchanged, Abel kicked the flanks of his horse and started down the path. Nicole's horse followed without any encouragement on her part. Thank goodness.

CHAPTER TWENTY-TWO

൚ ♦ ൙

The horses had followed the path for nearly thirty minutes before Nicole could see it. The only thing that differentiated it from the rest of the terrain was the fact that the places where the horses put their hooves had been smoothed out by years and years of travel. Those were only little sections here and there, but the horses seemed to know exactly where to step. She couldn't imagine walking this "path" on her own, without a horse. It would be pretty much impossible.

A few stars peeked through the clouds. Nicole found herself admiring the scenery—sure, it was rocky, dark, and a bit scary, but there was beauty in the ruggedness.

No one said anything for quite a while, and Nicole was okay with that. She was still uncomfortable with the Shiengol sitting directly behind her and could tell he did everything in his power not to touch her. She was grateful for that.

After about an hour, they reached what must have been the first fork. The trail to the right seemed to have more of the permanent hoof prints in it, while the way to the left obviously hadn't been traversed in a long time. The trees were thicker, their branches entwining together over the path, making it so travelers had to duck close to their horses to get through.

The next fork came twenty minutes after the first, and Nicole was relieved to find this part of the trail easier.

It seemed like hours before the third fork came, and Nicole drifted off over and over again. By the time they finally reached it, her stomach was growling loud enough for Azuriah to hear. He grunted in annoyance after every growl, which irritated Nicole in turn.

Luckily, both of the men were hungry too, so they stopped to take a break. Abel dismounted first, then helped Nicole off her horse, catching her off guard. While he didn't meet her eyes, she could sense a sort of compromise. He must've finally forgiven her for whatever it was that she did.

Their meal consisted of beef jerky, cheese, bread, and cold chicken broth. It was good, but Nicole knew she'd quickly tire of it.

Conversation was short, and Nicole found herself wishing Lizzie was there. She didn't regret her choice to leave her best friend behind, though.

Once they'd finished their meal, the three of them mounted the horses and continued onward. After about thirty more minutes, Abel pulled his horse up and glanced back at the other two.

"We're in the Great Ones' dimension now."

Nicole hadn't even realized they'd gone through the link because their surroundings looked exactly the same as they had before. She hoped Abel knew what he was talking about. Even if he didn't, Sanso had said they'd get there soon enough if they followed his directions, which they had.

Able urged his horse forward, and after a few minutes more, the cragginess of the trail gave way to smooth sand, and they started down narrow switchbacks into what looked like a deep and long valley. There was so much fog that Nicole wasn't sure where they were headed.

Abel pointed. "Those are the walls to the Great Ones' kingdom."

Nicole looked, straining her eyes, trying to see where he was pointing. All she saw were small mountains and rocky hills.

Able must've been able to tell she couldn't see because he said, "Don't worry. Your eyes will adjust soon."

As they continued down the switchbacks, Nicole watched as the area Abel had pointed to finally revealed something. A massive black wall jutted from the ground. How had Nicole not seen it before, and how had it been hidden? It was so obvious, so blatant.

The horses picked their way across the valley, following the trail, and those walls practically grew the closer the party got to them. They loomed over the entire valley. She understood why the Great Ones needed such huge walls. She hadn't been able to see anything other

WITHHOLD

than their legs the one time she'd met them.

Nicole wondered if she would see more of them now. Her fingers started to feel numb, despite the pleasant night air. Fear tingled down her back, making her heart beat erratically. This was either the bravest thing she'd ever done in her entire life, or the stupidest. Why had she volunteered? An even better question—why had it been *her* idea?

The closer they got to the doors, the more Nicole could sense the presence of other creatures, including magical beings. Their prints were different from hers. While her magic pulsed, these powers trickled through the air like sand. She couldn't tell if the magic she felt was from the Great Ones, or if it came from their servants.

The doors towered over them, casting huge shadows across the valley. At first, Nicole thought the wall was near, but as they continued following the trail, she saw it was large, large enough that the shadow it cast would take at least half an hour to cross.

Nicole couldn't help but stare at the wall as they approached. She could tell it was different, but she wasn't sure why.

Abel dismounted and approached the door on shaky legs. The poor man needed a year of food and rest, not more work.

As Abel stepped closer, Nicole gasped. The walls weren't made of wood, stone, or anything like that, but of living creatures. They shifted and roiled, tentacles reaching for him, faces and eyes appearing, staring at him. Sharp teeth jutted from the side of the wall, gnashing, trying to bite him. A tongue licked up his leg, and the creatures began howling.

Abel put his hands up, trying to quiet them. "It's all right, it's all right. You know me."

Nicole looked back at Azuriah. He met her gaze with a worried expression. She couldn't believe what they were up against. What would've happened if just she and the Shiengol had approached?

Abel stroked a few of the faces, blowing into the mouths and noses of many of the others, letting them catch his scent. He turned and glanced back at Nicole and Azuriah. "They recognize me, so we're good to go—at least, you are. I can't tell you how to reach the Great Ones from here, as I've never been beyond this point."

He turned to the doors again. "I am ready and willing to sacrifice my body to keep this door open while my guests visit the Great Ones' kingdom."

As soon as the words left Abel's mouth, a three-fingered hand snaked out and grabbed his arm. He shivered, an intense expression of distaste on his face. Many tentacles and other hands reached for him, grabbing him, pulling him close to the door. As soon as his whole body was in contact with the door, it slowly started opening.

Nicole and Azuriah dismounted, tethering their horse near Abel's. Once the door had opened far enough, they stepped through.

She didn't know what to expect when they got on the other side, but what greeted them definitely wasn't it.

The air was sticky and thick, difficult to breathe. Nicole's airways were quickly coated, and she couldn't help but cough to clear it. Little creatures floated through the air, squirming and wriggling. Nicole gasped, hands at her mouth, when she recognized several of them—or at least recognized their species. These were the things that had haunted her visions back when she and Austin weren't able to touch each other. It made sense, as she was now in the Great Ones' kingdom, that she'd find the sorts of creatures they'd sent to torment her.

Nicole and Azuriah had only been inside the walls for a few seconds when people rushed at them, grabbing their clothes, touching their arms, pleading for help. Nicole struggled to shrug them off, noticing Azuriah doing the same. She didn't know why these people were persisting. Was a trick of their masters, or did they really want help? She couldn't allow herself to wonder about their circumstances—too many other people needed her right then.

She and Azuriah got separated multiple times until he finally linked his arm through hers. They didn't have to ask where the Great Ones' palace was—it dominated the entire city, bigger even than the doors they'd just entered, sharp spikes jutting into the sky. Why hadn't they seen it over the walls? Perhaps the Great Ones had something rigged up that would prevent that.

The two of them followed the crooked and jagged streets toward the palace, multitudes of people still begging for help along the way. As they continued, Nicole recognized a few faces—Tarians, from when the great battle in Idaho had taken place.

Instead of feeling victorious over these people who had gotten their wish in such a bad way, Nicole felt only pity for them. They were so obviously miserable. She wondered if any of them recognized her too. So far, no one had said anything.

Then she heard something familiar—a woman's voice, calling her name over the sounds of people begging for freedom. Her heart began pounding so heavily inside her chest, she thought she would pass out. She pulled in several huge breaths, trying to control the fear and panic that nearly overwhelmed her the moment she spotted her great-great-grandmother.

CHAPTER TWENTY-THREE

Nicole hesitated, unsure of what to say. "Rebecca?"

The woman looked horrible. Her hair was knotted and messy, half of it clumped to her skull, the other half tumbling past her shoulders. Her clothes were dirty, ripped, and worn, sticking to her. Her face was gaunt, her eyes sunken in, dark rings around them, making her look like she'd been punched multiple times. Like everyone else, Rebecca clung to Nicole.

"What are you doing here?" Rebecca asked.

Nicole only shook her head. She didn't know if Rebecca still had any powers, but the less she knew of Nicole's plans, the better. She shrugged out of the woman's grasp.

"You won't leave this place," Rebecca said. "You

realize that, right? There's no way they'd allow it."

Nicole stopped trying to get away from the ghost. She met Rebecca's gaze, pondering what she'd just said. Her heart skipped a beat. Her grandmother was correct. The Great Ones *wouldn't* let her leave. That had been their promise—that if they ever ran across her again, she'd become their prisoner as well, or worse.

Crushing despair dropped on Nicole, making it hard to breathe. She allowed herself a moment of grief, thinking about the friends she'd left behind and the life with Austin she might never have. Then she squared her shoulders and said, "I'm willing to do what I must."

Then she turned her back on the woman, and arm still linked with Azuriah's, headed toward the palace again. The closer she and Azuriah got, the more diverse the creatures around them became. Several races Nicole had met from Jacob's world were there, including Shiengols, Makalos, and those little creatures that had run around Jacob, clambering for his attention. She couldn't remember what they were called. She also saw Molgs, Sindons, tons of Croents, and even a few Minyas.

She and Azuriah were nearly to the palace walls when the Great Ones recognized her. The connection between them must have still been active because she felt their shock at her coming, especially since they'd threatened her if they ever saw her again.

You need to hear what I know, she thought at them as hard as she could. She almost tagged on a plea that they release her after she delivered her message, but it felt like she'd be pushing her luck before they'd even granted her audience. The most important thing was them stopping

WITHHOLD

Keitus.

Nicole was grateful she was still holding on to Azuriah because the moment the Great Ones caught her thoughts, the streets around them disappeared, replaced by the insides of a *massive* room. This cathedral-like monstrosity had to be the palace. Pillars, the tops of which Nicole couldn't see, lined the room. Stained-glass window let in brilliant light. Little pews were arranged to face the front of the throne room, where Nicole found herself surrounded by what she assumed were huge legs.

The Great Ones were not happy to see her. She felt their displeasure, anger, and frustration all being directed toward her. The weight of the emotions was crushing, and she struggled to stay on her feet.

Little one, you realize the danger you've put yourself in by coming here?

Nicole recognized the thought as coming from the Great One she'd communicated with most during their last encounter. And even though the question was bordering on playful in tone, she knew a threat when she heard it. "Yes, but I have no choice."

Are we to trust what you have seen and heard? This thought came from a second Great One.

Obviously, they'd seen what was going on with Keitus in her mind. "Of course. But please, question Azuriah too."

The Shiengol looked at Nicole, fear on his face. She couldn't blame him. Just the size of the Great Ones was enough to cause fear. But the fact that they were huge *and* powerful was enough to make a weak person pass out from fright. Any idiot would be able to sense the magic that radiated from them. Knowing they created all of the powers in existence was just icing on the cake.

Well, Azuriah? The first Great One was back in charge of the conversation.

"What you've seen in Nicole's mind is the truth," he said. "I invite you to search my experiences as well."

The Great One chuckled, and the rumble made Nicole's heart feel funny.

A nice sentiment, considering we would have done it without your consent.

Nicole sensed the probing thoughts leave her mind and she felt it when they recognized the truth in Azuriah's. The curiosity and almost light-hearted feelings that had dominated the conversation were replaced with rage and fury.

Why have we not seen or heard of this?

Are we to be pushed over so often by our servants?

It is time we destroy what we have created. All magic must return to us.

No, the time has not come. We must allow them to continue.

Surely not this one.

Nicole saw Keitus in their thoughts.

The conversation between the Great Ones began going so rapidly that she could only catch brief snippets here and there. Their anger turned into determination, and they began plotting and planning. Nicole caught a bit of fear and that was followed by panic as the Great Ones recognized just how powerful Keitus had become. For the first time, she worried that they *couldn't* stop him. If the Great Ones were afraid, could Keitus destroy them?

WITHHOLD

She gasped when the Great Ones suddenly disappeared, leaving the room completely vacant. She looked at Azuriah, wondering if he and Nicole would be allowed to leave.

The moment the question was in her mind, though, Azuriah stiffened, his eyes glazing over. Tentacles sprang through the cracks in the stone floor, wrapping themselves around Nicole's legs and up her body, holding her in place. She shrieked for help, holding on to Azuriah's arm tightly. He didn't hear her. The tentacles stopped moving, and Nicole dragged in a breath, trying to control her panic.

Azuriah's gaze focused again and he began breathing heavily.

"Are you okay?" she whispered.

He didn't respond for a moment, then nodded, licking his lips, looking like he desperately needed water. "I—I—have been commanded to leave. I won't ever be able to return. You'll be here alone. I'm sorry, Nicole."

"Did they say what will happen to me?"

He nodded. "They've claimed you as their slave. They say they'll know the moment you try to leave, and they'll destroy you if you do."

Azuriah turned and grabbed both her arms. "I'm sorry for the way I've treated you. You are brave and good. You have fought hard for your loved ones, and even for people who despise you. You have fought hard for everyone."

"I'm sorry for my behavior too." Nicole was surprised when her voice didn't catch—she was struggling to hold back tears.

Azuriah gave her a small smile. "You don't need to apologize to me."

He opened his mouth to say something else, but before he could, he disappeared.

Nicole was alone.

The sticky, moist air was difficult to breathe. Her heart felt like it was pulsating inside her chest, like it was about to pop through her ribs at any moment. She looked around. Were the tentacles going to hold her here until the Great Ones returned?

Nicole gasped, sensing Onyev bestow guardianship status on Azuriah. She closed her eyes as a sudden relief rushed over her. She wouldn't have to bear the burden of Shonlin alone any longer. If she died, Azuriah would take up the task of protecting the magical forest. The relief that continued cascading down her head and back, making her skin tingle, told her just how stressed she'd been by that assignment.

If Azuriah had been granted guardianship status, he must be safe now. Nicole breathed another sigh of relief. She cocked her head—Azuriah hadn't exited the city the way he'd entered it. Was Abel still waiting for her? Did she have a chance? Would she be able to escape? Even if it meant sure death, she *had* to try because staying here definitely meant death.

Nicole startled when the tentacles hoisted her into the air, carrying her from the huge room. They took her down several flights of regular-sized stairs and into what appeared to be a dungeon. The cell they put her in was huge and had no furnishings. The tentacles released her, writhing their way back down the hall and presumably

WITHHOLD

up the stairs and to the throne room. The last of them shut the door with a loud, metallic clank before leaving.

Was she alone? No, she could sense other beings in the dungeon. She didn't want to take the time to find out if they were friendly or not.

She turned to the barred window opposite the cell door. It looked out over the rest of the kingdom, so the dungeon must have been on the second or third floor of the palace, judging by how high up she was.

Nicole heard the sounds of approaching footsteps and turned to face the cell bars. She groaned inwardly when she saw it was Rebecca.

The woman chuckled. "Who's a prisoner now?"

"How did you get in here?" Nicole asked.

"I might be a *servant* of the Great Ones," Rebecca said, "but they allow me freedom to move wherever I want in their kingdom." She narrowed her eyes, staring at Nicole. "You still have your powers, don't you?"

Nicole reached out to her magic. It was difficult to sense here, but it was there, ready and willing to help her. Could she break the wall down?

Rebecca seemed to see where Nicole's thoughts were taking her. "Don't try to escape. They'll just come find you again."

Why had the Great Ones allowed her to keep her magic? It didn't pulse the way it used to before she took the potion. Had the Great Ones sensed the change in her and assumed she was no longer magical? If so, why hadn't they said anything to that effect?

With just a brief touch of her thoughts to it, the sphere turned in Nicole's hand, out of sight of Rebecca.

The Great Ones hadn't taken it from her. Why not? Was Onyev's sealing that powerful?

"What do you want, Rebecca?"

Rebecca shrugged. "To torment you. To destroy your life the way you destroyed mine."

Nicole frowned. "I didn't do anything to you that wouldn't have happened anyway."

Rebecca opened her mouth to respond, but just then, the floor beneath them quaked, and an expression of terror flitted across the woman's face before being replaced with glee. She glanced at Nicole. "If I were you, I would hide." She cackled. "But then, you have nowhere to hide, do you?"

Rebecca scurried away, her footsteps fading until Nicole couldn't hear them anymore. She was left alone to face whatever approached.

CHAPTER TWENTY-FOUR

୫ɔ ✦ ଦ୫

The floor vibrated again. Nicole looked around the cell, but Rebecca was right—there weren't any hiding places. A cold sweat flooded over her. Anything that made Rebecca afraid would be something Nicole didn't want around.

She scurried into the corner of the room and squished her back into it, curling her legs up and holding them close. The vibrations in the floor grew stronger and stronger, and a massive pulse of magic pounded into her. She trembled in the corner for several moments before realizing that the most powerful beings in this dimension—the Great Ones—were already gone. Nicole might not be *physically* powerful, but she was now stronger than almost anything she'd met, magically. Was she powerful enough to defeat this new challenge?

Rather than cower in the corner, Nicole rose to her feet and strode to the center of her cell, arms relaxed at her sides. She took a deep breath and raised her chin. After everything she'd been through and done over the past couple of years, *this* she could handle. What could be worse than a Shoggoth?

She faced the huge hall, refusing to allow herself to feel intimidated or frightened by the vastness of the pulses that continued reverberating through the stone. The floor underneath quaked as the creature drew nearer. What exactly was it?

She didn't have to wait long to find out. The beast that stepped into view made her gasp. The torches that lined the huge hall illuminated what looked to be hundreds and hundreds of mangled human bodies pressed together, all smashed into one. They were shifting and moving, and for a moment, she wondered if they were alive. But no—they were completely lifeless, their bodies making up one huge monster.

Her lip curled in disgust as the creature stepped closer and she got a good look at it. The thing was covered with blood and gore. She shuddered. Hundreds of legs formed each of the monster's four legs. The arms were the same, but instead of legs, they were created by arms. The head was made up of tons and tons of heads from humans, all of them rolling and mashing and blending together. The eyes on the visible faces were open, staring in random directions. Even though they seemed lifeless, they blinked as one, as if they were being controlled by a single entity.

The beast took another step forward, and at once, all of the eyes focused on Nicole. A huge maw opened, and a great bellow emitted from it. Nicole felt herself getting pulled to the creature. She didn't have anything to hold on to, so she dropped to the floor, trying to grip the cold stone, using her shoes to push against the force that yanked her toward the beast. She wasn't strong enough to stop her forward momentum, though.

Changing tactics, Nicole pushed out with her magic, trying to control the dead bodies that made up the monster. They didn't respond. Were they not truly dead, then?

The force grew in strength until she slammed into the bars, her body being sucked toward the monster. The bars began cutting into her, the pressure so great that the wind was knocked out of her lungs.

Nicole screamed as she was pulled even harder into the bars. It didn't take much to realize that this beast probably had the magical strength to pull until her body broke enough to reach it.

About to black out from the pain, Nicole knew she had to do something to save herself. Not knowing whether her actions would backfire, Nicole sent her magic to the stone floor that supported the beast. She commanded it to collapse.

The resulting chaos was magnificent. The floor plunged downward, taking the monster with it. That wasn't the only thing that gave out—several pillars crashed down, along with the ceiling and most of the opposite wall.

Dust billowed up from the crevice, and Nicole heard people screaming and crying. The pressure pulling her against the bars stopped, and she jumped out of the way just as that entire wall plummeted into the hole.

The crying stopped.

Nicole cautiously stepped to the crevice and looked down. The parts of the beast still visible weren't moving. Was it dead? She wasn't going to stick around to find out. She looked up and down the hall, trying to figure out how to get out of her cell.

Taking care not to step on any cracks—she couldn't tell if the floor was safe where the cracks were—she walked to the right side of her cell and saw that a few bars had created a sort of bridge when they'd fallen. She used a little of her magic and coaxed the bars farther to the right to complete that bridge.

Nicole had never been a fan of heights, and she refused to look down as she stepped onto the bars. They weren't securely attached to anything. She teetered for a bit as she tried to keep her balance, then put a hand on the crumbling stone wall to her right, using her magic to encourage the bars not to move.

Slowly and carefully, she crossed to the stone floor on the other side. Once safe, Nicole slumped over, hands on her knees, breathing deeply. That had been way too close. Her body ached where she'd been pulled against the bars—she'd definitely bruise—and her heart seriously might never recover.

Nicole sensed as magical creatures started to head in her direction. They must've been attracted by the magic she'd used. She rushed down the hall, hoping to find a way out of the palace quickly. Who knew how long Abel would be able to hold the door open?

The palace was a maze of hallways, dead ends, and dungeons. Practically the entire thing was a dungeon.

WITHHOLD

Nicole eventually figured out that when the Great Ones left, the hold on their prisoners released, and most of the monsters were trying to escape. Nicole followed a set of fast little creatures that ran on claws, attacking anything they saw. They seemed to know where they were going, so she followed them, using her powers to sense when they turned corners, keeping out of sight.

Nicole's joy at getting out of the palace was short-lived—the streets were worse, much worse. A whole host of monsters had flooded them and were tormenting humans, and Nicole was quickly enveloped in the throng. She was jostled back and forth, her hair pulled, her skin scratched, and clothes yanked as she tried to make her way through the streets and to the door.

It seemed that the monsters were attracted to her because everywhere she went, they turned and looked. Was it because she was alive and the other humans were ghosts? *Were* they all ghosts? She couldn't tell, and she didn't want to take the time to find out.

Nicole battled her way physically by pushing, shoving, and shouldering. Several times, she was forced to use her magic to move creatures by grabbing them by their clothing and tossing them.

She held back as much as she could, paranoid that her magic would give out and she would be caught in a fight, unable to defend herself.

The familiar warmth from overdoing it never came. As a result, Nicole got more confident in her ability to push onward. At one point, the streets were so congested with monsters trying to stop her that she had to blow up everything in front of her, then use a whirlwind to plow a path through the debris. She shouldn't have been able to do that—her powers never would have lasted long enough before.

After she'd nearly reached the big wall, Nicole's body finally began to fail. It wasn't from magic, as she been expecting, but because of her lungs. The air was too thick. She wasn't getting enough oxygen and she started to wheeze, gagging and coughing. Her muscles were burning from oxygen starvation. Why was she struggling *now*? Nicole knew the answer even as she thought the question. She was pushing herself harder, using the oxygen in the air much quicker than she had been earlier.

She stumbled, picked herself up, forced her legs to continue carrying her forward. She was nearly to the door when something grabbed her, yanking her back. Rebecca. Was the woman following her? It wouldn't surprise Nicole if that was the case.

"You dare try to escape?" Rebecca asked. "Do you realize what will happen when they recognize you're gone?"

Nicole wheezed hard, the edges of her vision darkening as she gasped for air.

Rebecca laughed. "And again, I have the upper hand! You're unable to breathe here, aren't you? One of the benefits of being dead."

Nicole stumbled to her feet, not in the mood for a showdown with her evil ancestor. Forcing her exhaustion and dizziness aside, she grabbed Rebecca's arm. "I'm *never* at a disadvantage around you. I don't care what the reason is—if I ever feel your presence again, I swear, I will seek you out and destroy you."

WITHHOLD

Before Rebecca could respond, Nicole used her magic to hoist the woman by the clothes into the air and fling her across the city. Then she slumped to the ground, her energy spent.

CHAPTER TWENTY-FIVE

℘ ♦ ℘

She crawled forward, trying to force herself to calm down so she didn't need as much oxygen.

The door was within sight, Abel barely holding it open. Nicole started. No monsters were trying to stop her now. What was going on? Why weren't they bothering her? She looked back. The streets were nearly vacant now, and while she watched, a handful of monsters disappeared. Her mouth popped open. The Great Ones were calling them, pulling them to the battle to fight. Did that mean they actually needed help?

Nicole had to hurry—had to make it. She heard the sound of feet behind her and turned to see thousands of humans rushing at the door, obviously sensing that she was close to exiting. The anger on their faces left no doubt in her mind what they planned to do if they caught her.

WITHHOLD

She forced herself to her feet, pushed herself onward, toward the door. Getting away from the people now chasing her wasn't nearly as big a goal as finding a way to help the Great Ones win this battle. Filled with a burst of energy at the realization that the Great Ones might actually lose, she reached the door faster than she thought possible.

Abel didn't recognize her. He stared beyond her with eyes that were glazed over. His skin was ashen, his lips blue as he mouthed wordlessly. Nicole rushed to him, momentarily forgetting her own discomfort. How was he still holding the door open? Nicole wouldn't have been surprised if he didn't remember why he was keeping it from shutting.

By this point, the door had almost shut. She pushed herself through the six inches that were left, smashing Abel against the tentacles that held him as she passed. When she was through, she turned and grabbed his arm, yanking him free. He tripped after her, barely staying on his feet just as the hordes of people reached the wall.

The door slammed shut. Howling started up inside, and Nicole glanced at Abel.

"Will the doors hold?" she asked.

He stared at her, his lips moving as he tried to formulate an answer. "Yes . . . They're magically strengthened . . . by the Great Ones."

She decided not to bring up the fact that said Great Ones were no longer there, and that their prisons had actually started falling apart in their absence. Instead, she grabbed him by the hand and rushed to the horses that were still tethered, munching on the grass that lined the path. She helped Abel into his saddle, then jumped into her own, grateful that the air outside the Great Ones' kingdom was a little easier to breathe. She picked up the reins to Abel's horse and urged her horse into a run, pulling his alongside hers, rushing the way they'd come.

Nicole didn't slow until they'd reached the link back to the Ember Gods' dimension. The moment they passed through, she pulled her horse up and collapsed against it. Her ears began ringing and she nearly threw up, waiting for her body to adjust to the sudden increase of oxygen. Abel was unconscious in his saddle, and she herself barely stayed awake.

After a moment, knowing she couldn't rest for too long, Nicole urged the horses onward, letting them pick the pace now that they were traversing the rocky path again.

They hadn't gone far when Lizzie and Jacob rounded a corner. Nicole's stomach dropped as she watched her friends approaching, their feet heavily bandaged to protect against the sharp stones. Had they really followed her on foot?

"What on *earth* did you do?" Lizzie screamed the moment she saw it was Nicole. "Why did you leave us? We were supposed to help you! What would have happened if you'd gotten killed?"

She wasn't the only one who was upset. Jacob's face was purple from anger. He joined Lizzie in yelling at Nicole, and for a moment, she was so surprised, she didn't know what to say.

"I could have keyed you out of there! You didn't need to go alone—we could have waited at the wall for you!"

WITHHOLD

"Stop," she said loudly.

They ignored her.

"Enough!"

Still, nothing got through to them.

Finally, Nicole magically stopped the sound that was coming out of their mouths.

"Be quiet!" she said. "It's done. I *had* to go without you, and it has nothing to do with me wanting to protect you and *everything* to do with the fact that Azuriah is a Shonlin guardian and no one else was."

That piqued their curiosity. They obviously wanted to know what being a guardian had to do with anything, and she released her hold on their sound as she explained.

"Onyev told me that the only other guardian in my time is Azuriah. I knew, since he wasn't already a guardian when I met him, that he'd eventually have to face the Great Ones. I also knew that no one else would survive an interaction with them. How did I know this?" She wanted to make sure that her friends understood. "Because no one else is a guardian. The Great Ones collect slaves. They would have sensed you near their kingdom and pulled you to them."

"So, you *were* trying to protect me. Again." Lizzie folded her arms and glared at Nicole.

Nicole slumped in her saddle. "Yes, but for good reasons." She hopped off the horse, wanting to be on the same level with her best friend. "Their entire kingdom is full of humans they've enslaved. A monster made up of hundreds and hundreds of human bodies nearly killed me—they would *not* have released you."

"They let you go," Jacob said, the purple in his face

fading to a light pink.

"Not really—they'll probably call me right back once we help them win the war."

Lizzie tilted her head. "*Help* them? Why would they need help? Wasn't that the whole point of getting them to come—because they could do it and we couldn't?"

Nicole nodded. "Yes, but I'm afraid Keitus is too powerful. Right as I was leaving the Great Ones' city, monsters began disappearing left and right. I think the Great Ones were pulling them to the battle. And if they need recruits, they're not winning."

Jacob's eyes clouded over as he Time-Saw through the dimensions, probably looking for evidence that what Nicole was saying was true. It didn't take him long to come back. "You're right. It doesn't look good. I was only watching you—I didn't even think to see what was going on with Keitus once the Great Ones had gone. I just assumed they would take care of him."

Lizzie turned to him. "What's happening?"

"It looks like Keitus has relinquished his hold on all the worlds but earth. Unfortunately, he's somehow staying ahead of the Great Ones there. I think he may have killed some of them. Only one is left fighting him."

Nicole's eyes widened. "How is that possible?"

"I don't know. We should go, though I don't know how we're supposed to help."

Nicole could only shake her head. She didn't know either. "Let's head back to Sanso's. See if anyone can come fight with us—we're going to need as many magical people as possible."

Lizzie nodded, then turned to follow the path, but

WITHHOLD

Nicole stopped her. "Get on Abel's horse, Lizzie, and Jacob, hop up with me. The horses know these paths well—we should let them do the work while we rest." Nicole wished she could ride with her best friend, but Jacob and Abel were too close in weigh, and Lizzie practically weighed nothing.

The others did as she suggested, and they headed out.

"What I can't understand," Lizzie said, "is why Keitus relinquished his hold on Eklaron. Why is he only controlling earth? Isn't he *from* Eklaron?"

"Yes," Jacob said. "I suspect it's because he was still on earth when the Great Ones found him. It's easier to protect a place when you're physically there."

"Where on earth are they?" Nicole asked.

Jacob and Lizzie both laughed, and Nicole chuckled. "Okay, I wasn't even trying to make a joke. You know what I'm asking, though."

"It looked like somewhere in Kansas or maybe Oklahoma," Jacob said. "The Great Plains, for sure."

The four hours back to Sanso's were agonizingly long, even with Nicole drifting off every now and then. Since Azuriah had been the one carrying the food, and Lizzie and Jacob had been too mad to think about packing supplies when they started out after Nicole, they were starving as well.

Nicole was relieved to see Sanso's cabin. She gasped when she saw Austin standing in the doorway, a worried expression on his face.

Throwing herself from the horse, then immediately wishing she hadn't done so, Nicole lurched and limped through the stones to her fiancé. She wanted to throw

176

herself into his arms, but couldn't—not until she knew how he was feeling.

His arm was in a sling, and a huge bandage was on his head. Nicole felt tears pool in her eyes as she inspected him.

"How are you doing?" she asked, hoping he wasn't going to yell at her too.

Austin grunted. "Better, now that I know you're not dead or dying in the Great Ones' dimension somewhere."

He didn't seem mad, and Nicole placed a kiss on his lips. "They need help. We're going to get a bunch of healthy people to go fight."

Austin glowered, catching the meaning behind her words. "I don't have to be physically strong to fight with magic."

"I know. But just in case. You've lost way too much blood—you're very pale."

"If I feel sick, I'll play dead, I promise. If I don't come now, I'll just have Sanso help me find a different way."

The expression in his eyes told Nicole there was no way he'd stay behind, and she smiled at him, a bit relieved to know she wasn't going to be separated from him again. She glanced behind him as Hayla walked down the hall. "How's your husband doing?" she called to the woman.

Hayla proceeded to give updates on everyone. Coolidge was still unconscious, but his condition had stabilized. Dmitri was awake and cracking jokes, but a broken leg prevented him from going anywhere. Arien had been stabbed in the shoulder but was also doing

WITHHOLD

fine—nothing important had been cut. Most had been wounded, some gravely, but none had actually lost their lives.

After a brief counsel with Dmitri, Austin, Nicole, and Lizzie, Jacob started creating links to all the different dimensions and worlds where they knew they had allies. Apparently, Dmitri had been sending messages everywhere, contacting friends, asking them to gather together so Jacob could key them to earth to help in the battle. Supporters were waiting on Renforth's planet, Eklaron, and in Anna Morse's dimension. Even the Fire Pulsers' world had a few people willing to fight.

Jacob kept those links open, letting people pour from their worlds and dimensions and congregate in Sanso's little house. It quickly got too crowded, and he opened links to the castle in Eklaron too, which had been deserted by Keitus's armies when he'd pulled out of that world. While people continued gathering, Nicole walked to the kitchen, knowing she needed food and to rest before she could go to earth. Jacob, Austin, and Lizzie followed her, and they sat together to eat. Conversation was short—no one was in the mood for small talk.

Once he'd finished eating, Jacob Time-Saw to earth and came back with good news—Keitus and the Great One had momentarily stopped fighting and were regrouping, which meant that Nicole and the others would have a little time to sleep.

Nicole stuffed herself as full as she could, hoping the extra food would induce a sleep coma, then she and Lizzie went to their little room to rest.

CHAPTER TWENTY-SIX

☯ ◆ ☙

What felt like only moments later, Austin was shaking her awake. He placed a gentle kiss on her lips.

"Jacob says it looks like Keitus and the Great One will start fighting soon. It's time for us to head out."

Nicole pulled herself to a sitting position. "You should have been sleeping," she said.

He shook his head. "I've had plenty of it lately."

"Good." She got to her feet and gave him a hug.

Lizzie was awake by then, and the three of them met Jacob back in the kitchen. He'd found an old wheat factory a few miles from where everything was happening back on earth. He opened a link from the bone dimension and from Sanso's home to that location.

While watching volunteers stream through the links to earth, he turned to Nicole and said, "By a few miles, I really mean fifteen." Worry lines deepened on his forehead. "If we make it there before Keitus destroys that last Great One, it'll be a miracle."

Nicole frowned, doing the math in her head. "Fifteen miles will take us three hours to walk. We can do it, if we hurry."

She watched for a moment as tons of creatures poured through the links, then she turned to her friends. Austin put his good arm around her and sent her a smile. Lizzie had already gotten over her frustrations. The girl never held grudges for long—Nicole was so grateful for that.

Nicole and her friends went through the link to the factory. The place was teaming with magical people. She could sense all kinds of magic flowing through the air. It was invigorating.

Once everyone who'd answered Dmitri's call for help, including Aretes from Nicole's dimension, had gathered, Jacob closed all of the links. They didn't want any of the "bad guys" to find a way back to Sanso's planet, regardless of how confident Sanso was that monsters couldn't set foot on his world. Besides, there were plenty of bad humans fighting on Keitus's side.

The link to Sanso's world had only been closed for a moment when the building shook, and Nicole heard the sounds of battle outside. She and the others stepped out, ready for whatever would greet them.

Her eyes widened as she took in the scene. Many of the people Jacob had brought were already battling—she hadn't even realized they'd left the wheat factory. Apparently, Keitus had sensed their approach and sent monsters to stop them. The entire countryside was covered with monsters, Aretes, humans, Shiengols, and all sorts of other creatures, fighting. There wasn't even a tree or house to block the view of the raging battle.

Nicole and Lizzie looked at each other. Would they have to fight the entire fifteen miles? If so, how long would that take?

"Let's go," Jacob said to Nicole. "I already know you plan to attack Keitus directly. We need to get to him as fast as we can."

Nicole nodded, then she, Austin, Jacob, and Lizzie rushed through the fighting monsters, knowing that their allies would stay behind and take care of the lesser beings. Nicole didn't want to have to run the entire fifteen miles, but she also didn't want to fight and turn those miles into two days.

Lizzie used the umbrella and focused on stopping and starting fires to the best of her ability while Austin dumped huge mud piles on monsters or formed rocks around their ankles. He also flung stones and sharp sticks at the beasts, clearing a path. Jacob used his magical shield to protect their group from attacks while Nicole used her Wind and Water powers to push and fling away monsters. Fighting like this, they charged on.

The farther they went, the more Nicole realized her powers had changed significantly. She still hadn't reached her threshold. Did she even have one anymore? If so, where was it? Or had her powers changed so much that overdoing it would produce a completely different symptom? Had she already overdone it, and was she doing permanent damage in some way? She didn't think so. If she was, wouldn't she have collapsed or experienced a loss in power?

WITHHOLD

The battle raged on either side of them. It was so deafening, Nicole could no longer hear when her friends talked. Guns were firing, swords clanged and flashed in the sunlight, and people roared battle cries or screamed in pain.

Lizzie's magic gave out ten minutes after they started running. Then Austin's. Nicole and her group were forced to slow—they couldn't run the entire time. She pushed out with her powers, still using her abilities to keep monsters away, and sensed that those who fought against Keitus were tiring, faltering, unable to keep up. She had to do something!

Austin touched her arm as they walked. "You still haven't reached your magical threshold, have you?"

She shook her head. What a difference from when she'd first Restarted! "I'm a Silver now, and it's Keitus's fault."

A wide grin spread across Austin's face. "That's fantastic. I'll bet he didn't expect it."

"Definitely not."

Nicole slowed, trusting Jacob to keep the shield around her and the others while she did something to help the people who were fighting. She followed the magical prints around her, recognizing the ones who were tied back to Keitus, then singling out those who weren't. Once sure she had a hold on the good guys, she lifted them by their clothes and armor, pulling them out of reach of the monsters and demons. Several screamed, not knowing what was going on. Nicole caved in the earth under the evil monsters. Before the demons could climb out of the hole, she sent a massive wave of dirt after them, covering them.

Then she flattened the ground again so she could put the people down, allowing them to rest or find more monsters to fight.

Once finished, she started running again. Nicole smiled sheepishly at the expressions of awe on her friends' faces. She herself was a bit in awe over how much her powers had improved.

She had to lift and smash several more times before they neared Keitus and the Great One, alternating running, walking, and resting the whole way. Eventually, they were barely able to walk at all. And still, the battle raged. How was it possible that there were so many monsters and creatures available to fight?

Finally, several hours after they started, Nicole and the others reached Keitus and the Great One. Nicole sensed the mental print of this being immediately. It was the one who always communicated with her, the most powerful of them all. But he was smaller now, much smaller—only a little bigger than Keitus. What had happened?

The Great One was weary and barely recognized Nicole as she and her friends arrived. She figured that if he had chosen to comment at that point, he probably would've scoffed at the meager help they offered.

But Keitus recognized the threat immediately. He turned to them, saw Jacob and Nicole, and growled loudly enough that the monsters around them stopped fighting. The area was so full of dead bodies. How were they even fighting at all?

She recognized the advantage this gave her, though.

WITHHOLD

She might be able to use those bodies against Keitus. Not like zombies—she couldn't give them life—but as a way to hedge his movements.

Keitus had other plans, though, and Nicole had to wonder if he could read her mind. Before she was able to do anything to stop him, Austin grabbed her by the throat.

"Don't you dare go through with your plan," he said.

Nicole choked, trying to get his hand off her neck. He wasn't the only one Keitus was controlling. Lizzie and Jacob were both lifeless, the light gone from their eyes. Why was Keitus controlling them and not her?

When Austin responded, Nicole knew for sure that Keitus could hear her thoughts.

"The sphere protects you from my control."

Nicole was surprised at first that he would tell her something like that, then her eyes widened as she considered his words. Had Onyev known the sphere could protect her from being manipulated by Keitus? He must have.

"If you do anything," Austin said, "I will kill him."

Nicole knew Keitus was referring to Austin. "It doesn't matter. You have to be stopped—regardless of the consequences."

Not waiting for Keitus to respond, Nicole grabbed all the dirt she could carry, mixing it with dead bodies and shrubbery and weeds and everything that was within her magical sight. She lifted it, then slammed it on and around Keitus. The Great One joined her, smothering Keitus with debris and wind and rain.

Keitus didn't fight back nearly as much as Nicole

thought he should for how powerful he was. He was just as exhausted as the Great One. The fact that both of them were still standing was a miracle.

Austin's grip around Nicole's neck tightened, but she reached up and grabbed his fingers, trying to pry them away while using her power to yank him from her by his clothes. She cried out as his hand slipped off her neck.

No longer being held back, Nicole focused all her attention on stopping Keitus. She stepped forward, her body so exhausted that it wanted to collapse. But she couldn't stop now, not when they were so close.

She needed to protect her thoughts from him. What could she do? Did Shonlin have a magical item that functioned like that?

The sphere appeared in her hand. Nicole created a huge windstorm, spiraling it tightly around her to protect her from attack, then she imagined herself in Shonlin.

"What do you need?" the guardian asked immediately, his face strained—did he know what was going on? He had to.

"Something that can protect my thoughts from outside influences, including the ability to know what I'm thinking."

The guardian nodded, then took her to the appropriate shelf. The item wasn't at all what she expected—it was a sheet of stickers. She raised an eyebrow, looking at him.

"Put one in a secure location. It'll do what you need."

"I only need one?"

"Yes."

"Then I'll leave the sheet here."

She didn't want to risk ruining the others—not when

WITHHOLD

she was in the middle of a battle.

Nicole chose a little bluebird sticker and put it near her heart, under her shirt. Then she exited the room and dropped the whirlwind.

She was ready to face Keitus.

CHAPTER TWENTY-SEVEN

☙ ◆ ❧

Nicole sensed it the moment his mind was torn from hers. She didn't even realize how much he'd invaded her head. A sense of aloneness nearly overwhelmed her for a moment before she was able to shake it off and press forward with her senses, searching for the talisman.

She left her friends behind, trusting they would be safe, but realizing that even if they weren't, she had to continue.

Where was that stupid talisman? Her magic couldn't sense any of it on him. Why hadn't the Great One already removed it? It had to be because the Great One couldn't get close enough. But she could—she was small and fast.

She was fifteen feet from him, but that was still closer than she'd ever been, and he was much more grotesque

WITHHOLD

and disgusting than she'd seen earlier. His skin was so swollen and stretched so tightly and thinly that it was ripping in places.

Keitus held a huge sword in one hand while trying to dig himself out of the mess Nicole had created with the other. He sent occasional jabs at the Great One. His attempts were pathetic, but the Great One's attempts to defend himself were just as pathetic.

Both ignored Nicole. The Great One continued attacking Keitus with magic, and Nicole finally got close enough to sense the talisman. It was tied around one of his ankles. She hesitated. Why was it there?

Nicole looked up at Keitus as he struggled against the next onslaught of debris from the Great One. He must not have expected anyone to look there for it. It was a good plan—she would have gone for his neck first.

She raced up the pile of debris where Keitus was trapped. The leg that had the talisman was covered. When she got close enough, Nicole dug in with her hands and magic, pulling the dirt and debris aside, ignoring the things she was having to touch to reach him. Finally, she got to his ankle.

Just as she reached for it, though, Keitus freed himself and stepped down on her arm, glaring at her.

Nicole screamed as her bones snapped. Keitus ground his foot harder, probably pulverizing her arm completely. Her vision blackened, then came back just as the Great One physically attacked Keitus, pushing him over with a massive foot.

Keitus toppled down the side of the hill away from Nicole. Using her good arm, she pulled herself to her feet. Her right arm was a mess—she knew it was. She couldn't bring herself to look at it. The pain alone almost made her pass out. But she had to get to Keitus! Had to remove that talisman.

Nicole stumbled down the hill after Keitus. She sent a mental message to the Great One to explain what she was doing, but the little sticker prevented the Great One from accessing her thoughts as well. *That* would have been handy a long time ago.

She lost her balance and fell, screaming out as she instinctively used her injured arm to catch herself.

"Oh, my gosh, oh, gosh," she panted, trying to breathe through the pain.

Keitus and the Great One continued fighting. Nicole's friends were still in a daze behind her, not moving. Had he wiped their minds?

She struggled forward, using her left arm to pull herself toward her target.

Keitus was grappling with the Great One. Through the haze caused by her pain, Nicole recognized something—the more Keitus attacked and swiped at the Great One with his sword, the smaller the Great One became as chunks of him fell off. He was still functional, but nowhere near as strong as he had been before. Instead of a monstrous being hundreds of feet tall, this version of the Great One was only about twenty feet tall. His chin was made up of huge tentacles that waved madly. He had several eyes, all of them focused on Keitus.

Nicole continued forward.

She got close enough to reach the talisman, but Keitus again stepped away. And again, Nicole was forced to

WITHHOLD

follow.

Finally, in a last-ditch effort, she lunged for it. Her broken arm slammed against his body, causing waves of pain and nausea to flood through her as she held on as tightly as she could with her good hand. She screamed and used her magic to break the string that held it around his ankle. With a snap, the cord broke, and Nicole tumbled backward. This time, she didn't try to stop her fall.

Keitus teetered around, narrowly missing stepping on Nicole. She watched as he underwent a huge transformation. Massive chunks fell from him as he shed the immortal, deadly form.

Soon, nothing was left but the ghost of the shriveled old man.

And the Great One promptly destroyed that ghost with a blast of magic so bright, Nicole had to look away.

With a groan of exhaustion, the Great One stooped and took the talisman from Nicole, totally ignoring her. He peered at the talisman for a moment, then directed another powerful wave of magic to it, obliterating it into a million shiny pieces.

With a single nod to Nicole, the Great One brought himself upright, then disappeared.

All sounds of the battle around Nicole ceased. Monsters that had been fighting for Keitus glanced around in confusion, obviously wondering what happened to their master.

Nicole watched with a smile as Austin, Lizzie, Jacob, and Akeno rounded the hill. They spotted her just as she blacked out.

CHAPTER TWENTY-EIGHT

༄ ♦ ༄

When Nicole awoke, she was inside a Minya container. She pushed the lid back, happy to see that Austin on the other side. She knew this place—it was the castle in Maivoryl City. Nicole pulled herself to her feet, inspecting herself as she did so. Her right arm had been healed without evidence of any injury. The bruises that had been forming from the bars in her cell were gone, as were all the little scratches, burns, scrapes, and cuts she'd received over the past several days.

She seriously *loved* Kaede sap.

Austin's head was nodding as he struggled to stay awake, one hand on the table where her container had been situated. She stepped out of the container and crossed the table, patting his hand.

"Hey," she said.

Austin jumped, blinking rapidly. "You're awake!"

He held his hand out for her and she hopped onto it, grabbing his thumb. Austin carried her to Akeno, who enlarged her. The moment she was back to her normal size, she ran to Austin, throwing her arms around him.

"I don't care what anyone says," Austin said. "We're getting married right now."

Nicole chuckled. "Well, let's at least send invitations and see who can come."

Austin gave her a wicked grin. "Don't need to."

Just then, Lizzie and Queen Arien entered the room holding a wedding gown, veil, and a beautiful bouquet of red roses, white daisies, vines, and baby's breath. Nicole noticed for the first time that Austin was wearing a tux.

She gasped. "Now?"

His grin widened. "Yes. I'm not letting you out of my sight until you're mine. If that's okay with you, of course."

She jumped into his arms, squealing. "Yes, yes! It's perfect with me."

Austin and Akeno left so Lizzie and the queen could help Nicole get into the wedding dress. It fit her perfectly, and Nicole couldn't help but wonder how they'd known her size—Lizzie didn't remember her own size, let alone Nicole's.

Lizzie saw her confused expression and giggled. "We might have raided your closet in Texas. Well, *we* didn't—my mom did."

"Your mom is here?"

"Yup! She, Dad, my brothers, and your brothers are waiting in the throne room."

Warmth and happiness spread through Nicole at

everything her friends had done to fulfill her dream wedding. And she couldn't believe they'd pulled this all off while she'd been healing!

Queen Arien and Lizzie helped do her hair and makeup. While they were finishing up, Elyse, Dave's mom, entered carrying a beautiful necklace and a pair of earrings. She gave them to Nicole, then enveloped her in a big hug.

"I'm so excited," she whispered.

Coolidge came in next, wearing a tux. Nicole threw her arms around him. "I'm glad to see you alive and doing well."

He smiled. "You have a choice to make."

"What's that?"

"Who's going to give you away to Austin?"

Nicole chuckled. "You are, of course. Who else would do it?"

"I was hoping you'd say that."

After the women deemed Nicole ready, Coolidge held out his arm, Nicole took it, and he led her through the halls of the castle and into the most magnificent throne room she'd ever seen. Stained-glass windows graced nearly every wall, the floors and pews were marble, and beautiful lacy arches made up every doorway. Where had this room been hiding, and why wasn't Dmitri using it?

Coolidge walked Nicole down the aisle, and her heart fluttered at the sight of Austin at the other end, looking hot in his tux and wearing an expression of pride and contentment on his face.

She saw everyone she'd grown to care about for the past few years, smiling at her. The old ladies from

WITHHOLD

her apartment were near the back, sitting next to Sam, her landlord. Sylvia, Professor Nelson, his wife, and the Makalos were present. Albert and Prudence were in the middle, and Lizzie's family and Nicole's siblings were near the front. Azuriah, Pambri, and a few other Shiengols were there, scattered throughout the room. Even Judith Ann had shown up.

The audience was also made up of many people Nicole didn't know—one guy in particular, a man in his forties wearing light blue jeans and a brown leather jacket, caught her attention. He was vaguely familiar. He sent a smile before turning to talk to the woman with him. Nicole put him from her mind.

Coolidge gave Nicole to Austin, then sat next to Hayla and the Fat lady on the front row near Lizzie, Jacob, and Jacob's parents.

Nicole almost panicked. She didn't have any vows prepared. But Aldo, who was officiating at the wedding, reassured her with a smile and whispered, "Just say 'I do' at the appropriate part if you're sure you really want to marry him."

She chuckled—of course she wanted to. Knowing what was expected of her, she relaxed and enjoyed her wedding. Austin's expressions of pure adoration melted her heart and made her toes curl in anticipation. She couldn't believe they were finally getting married.

The day ended with a huge meal. It was undoubtedly the best wedding feast that had been seen in a long time—possibly since the king and queen themselves had been married.

Once the celebration ended, Nicole and Austin

changed into street clothes, then Austin led Nicole to where a Sindon awaited them near the castle doors. He picked her up, nestling her against his chest, and carried her up a ladder propped against the huge beast. Nicole wrapped her arms around his neck, snuggling against him, breathing deeply of the smell she knew and loved that made up her husband.

Husband.

She was *married* to Austin. Her heart jumped in her chest. She couldn't believe they'd finally made it to this day.

Austin tucked Nicole next to him on the bench, putting his arms around her, his warm brown eyes searching her face. "Nicole, I couldn't say this earlier—too many people present—but every happiness and hope I carry now can be traced back to my decision to choose you. To date you and to love you. You are my present and my future, and I will love you forever."

Nicole blinked back tears that pricked her eyes. She pulled him close, her arms tightening around him. How could she respond to such eloquence? She'd never been good with words. "I'm so glad you chose me over Savannah."

Austin pulled back, a confused expression on his face. "Savannah who?"

Nicole started explaining but saw the twinkle in his eyes and laughed, smacking his shoulder. "You tease. Fine, we won't talk about her." She settled against him again. "I love you too."

A simple response, but Austin's reaction to it helped her know it was the right one.

WITHHOLD

They honeymooned in a private cottage near a small lake that Arien and Dmitri owned.

☙ ♦ ❧

Nicole and Austin had only been home from their honeymoon for a week when she and Lizzie held a baby shower for Hayla. The event went well, and Nicole enjoyed spending time with the women around her. Her life had changed permanently—she'd gone from having a family that hated and despised her to becoming part of an accepting and loving one. She hadn't yet discovered a new threshold to her powers, and hoped she wouldn't ever have to. Opportunities to use her magic defensively were extremely rare now.

She finished her education, and she and Austin graduated at the same time. Lizzie had graduated the year before, doing what she loved—stopping fire—and had taken an internship in California, where she was learning to become a Fire Impeder.

Nicole and Austin moved to his family ranch in Montana, where she planned to spend as much of her time—and money—as possible.

Life was good.

EPILOGUE

Several years later.

Nicole brushed her hair out of her eyes, taking a break from pulling weeds in her garden. She wasn't physically pulling the weeds, of course—that was what her magic was for, and she'd gotten very fast at it. As a result, they'd had a huge garden every year since she and Austin had moved to Montana.

A shadow appeared next to her, and she startled, looking up. A man stood over her, wearing light blue jeans and a brown leather jacket.

She frowned. "You came to my wedding."

The man tilted his head, staring at her. "How did you remember that?"

"You were wearing this back then too," she said, gesturing at his clothes.

WITHHOLD

The man flushed, looking at his attire. "Oh, yeah. You're right."

"What do you need?" She knew this wasn't just a casual visit. Thank goodness the feeling around him was one of familiarity and friendship, not hostility.

"It's time you remembered. You must visit your mother and ask her where your old music box went."

Nicole frowned. "What are you talking about? What music box?"

"The one your grandmother gave you as a child."

Nicole nodded, vaguely remembering it. "Why do I need to visit my mom?"

"Because she was commanded to keep it safe."

"You know she's in prison, right?"

Tiffany had at least six or seven years left of her fifteen-year sentence. Nicole still thought she got off too easy.

"Yes. Go now. I'll come visit again once you've seen her."

Nicole tilted her head, wondering why she trusted him. It was as if they'd worked together—as if she'd known him very well at some point. But when? And how?

She followed his instructions immediately, arranging for the family helicopter to take her into town to the airport where their private jet waited. Having access to over a billion dollars made life much easier at Shadow Valley Ranch.

The flight to the prison where Tiffany was being held was hard on Nicole's already-troubled stomach. She hadn't gone to see her mother once since the woman had been locked up. And seeing her now, she was surprised at how awful Tiffany looked. Her hair had lost its shine, deep lines covered her face, and her eyes were dull and lifeless.

Nicole almost felt bad for the woman before realizing that yes, she'd forgiven her, but that didn't mean she had to forget what she had done.

"What do you want?" Tiffany asked.

Nicole's stomach turned at the sound of her mother's voice. She hadn't heard it in so long. Her stomach turned for other reasons too and she put a hand there, quieting the bubbles that were a constant companion these days.

"I need my old music box."

Tiffany narrowed her eyes. "Why now?"

Nicole hesitated, then decided to ignore the question. "Where is it?"

Her mother laughed. "You still don't know what happened, do you?"

Nicole didn't know how to respond, but she didn't have to because Tiffany continued. "It's in storage at the house. I locked it up in your father's gun safe in the basement."

Tiffany abruptly got to her feet, stepping away from Nicole. "Don't come here again. You've already ruined my life enough."

With that, the woman turned and left the room.

Nicole slowly stood and exited the prison, her thoughts swirling around her. What did Tiffany mean?

With only one passenger, it wasn't hard to arrange a trip to the airport outside of Lucas, Texas, and it didn't take long to get to her family's estate. Their old butler and housekeeper still lived there, and the housekeeper gave Nicole a hug.

Nicole didn't know the combination to the lock on the

WITHHOLD

gun safe, but she didn't need to. Her magic was able to show her which way to turn the dial. She opened the door and slid ammo boxes, pistols, revolvers, and rifles around until she found the little music box in a very back corner.

Nicole pulled it out. She heard a sound and whirled. The man was standing there, watching her. "Geez! Are you trying to freak me out? How did you get in here, anyway?"

He shook his head, but didn't respond to her questions. Instead, he started mumbling words. A sudden headache pounded into Nicole's skull. She gasped as memories flooded her system.

She remembered the man. His name was Alexander, and they had worked together years earlier, while she'd been in high school. Other memories flooded her mind. They were hazy and hard to grasp. Dogs shifting into humans, a horrible, creepy manor, an ex-boyfriend, and a prophecy.

A prophecy about Lizzie.

"I . . ." Nicole put a hand to her head. "I—I remember you."

Alexander nodded. "The rest of your memories will fall into place over the next couple of days."

She couldn't help but single out the one about her best friend. "There's a prophecy! About Lizzie! She's in danger!"

Alexander nodded.

"I have to get to her," Nicole said.

"Yes, you do. Immediately."

THE END

NOTE FROM THE AUTHOR

Have you already read *Forsake*? If not, make sure you check it out so you can learn exactly what it was that Alexander made Nicole forget. (Hint, it has to do with Lizzie, if you couldn't tell, ha ha. :-) Another hint: it's one of my bestest, most creepiest books yet. I had sooo much fun writing it! I can't wait to hear what you think of it. :-))

Also, *The Shade Amulet, Koven Chronicles Book One* will be coming out soon. That's the first book in Lizzie's series. Join my readers group to be alerted to its release! It's going to rock! And if you're reading this book, I think it's safe to say you're a reader of mine. :-)

To my devoted and loyal readers: I'm so sorry it took so long to get this book to you. It's one of the hardest books I've ever written. A lot of you know I had an accident at home where the device storing this book got destroyed. $700 later, I had the book in my possession again, but my emotions were shot from the experience of having it get lost. As a result, I really struggled with finishing it. Instead, I wrote *Forsake*—the book that delves into Nicole's experiences with Alexander—and *The Shade Amulet*, Lizzie's first book, finally getting back to *Withhold* over six months after I'd started it.

I hope you enjoyed the ending of the Mosaic Chronicles. It felt good to dip my toes back into Jacob and Nicole's worlds for a little while, but I think I am done with both of them—I feel like their stories are complete now.

If you want to know when I release my next book (and there's no way I'm done writing fantasy and magic!), make sure you become a member my readers group (as if you're surprised I was going to say that :-)), where you can get free stories and lots of fun stuff. More information on my website! www.andreapearsonbooks.com

Thank you! And as always, much love!

Andrea

P.S. Help my books take flight! Please leave reviews. I'll love you forever even more if you do. :-)

Andrea Pearson, author of several series including the Kilenya Chronicles, Kilenya Romances, and the Mosaic Chronicles, lives with her husband and children in a small valley framed with hills. She graduated from Brigham Young University with a bachelor of science degree in Communications Disorders.

Andrea spends as much time with her husband and kids as possible. Favorite activities include painting, watching movies, collecting and listening to music, and discussing books and authors.

To learn more about Andrea, visit her website at www.andreapearsonbooks.com

Made in the USA
Las Vegas, NV
28 January 2025